From: Alice Madigan
Sent: 1st February 09:00
To: Liam Conway
Subject: Strictly business?

Liam:

I can't believe that you are my new boss—I'm so embarrassed! Of course I promise to keep things strictly business from now on...

Alice

From: Liam Conway
Sent: 1st February 09:00
To: Alice Madigan
Subject: The boss's proposal...

Hi Alice

Boardroom meeting in ten—just to formally introduce myself...

How about dinner at eight?

Liam

Barbara Hannay was born in Sydney, educated in Brisbane, and has spent most of her adult life living in tropical North Queensland, where she and her husband have raised four children. While she has enjoyed many happy times camping and canoeing in the bush, she also delights in an urban lifestyle—chamber music, contemporary dance, movies and dining out. An English teacher, she has always loved writing, and now, by having her stories published, she is living her most cherished fantasy. Visit www.barbarahannay.com

Recent titles by the same author:

THE CATTLEMAN'S ENGLISH ROSE*
THE BLIND-DATE SURPRISE*
THE MIRRABROOK MARRIAGE*
CHRISTMAS GIFT: A FAMILY

*Southern Cross trilogy

HAVING THE BOSS'S BABIES

BY
BARBARA HANNAY

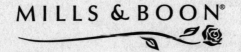

MILLS & BOON®

First published in Great Britain 2005
Paperback Edition 2006
Harlequin Mills & Boon Limited,
Eton House, 18-24 Paradise Road, Richmond, Surrey TW9 1SR

© Barbara Hannay 2005

ISBN 0 263 84881 7

Set in Times Roman 10½ on 12¼ pt.
02-0206-42169

Printed and bound in Spain
by Litografia Rosés, S.A., Barcelona

CHAPTER ONE

SHE was sitting alone at the bar with her back to him, so he wasn't sure why she caught his attention. Perhaps it was because she seemed so different from the rest of the under-thirty-fives who packed the Hippo Bar for Friday-night cocktails. No laughter or mad flirting for her.

She was staring at her empty cocktail glass, stirring what was left of the ice cubes with a tiny black straw, oblivious to the happy commotion going on all around her.

Her clothes were different, too. No tight hipster jeans or bare midriff, no outrageous jewellery or spangly glitter.

Her shiny dark hair was caught up in a simple knot and her dress, something dark and feminine with one shoulder bare, offered a clear view of the graceful line of her neck and shoulders. Her skirt wasn't especially short but it managed to reveal rather shapely legs.

He wanted to see her face; if it matched the rest of her it was, at the very least, elegant.

And then, miraculously, she turned and his lungs compressed as if he'd free-dived to the bottom of the Coral Sea. She was quite, quite lovely.

Her eyes were clear grey, her nose classic and her mouth lush. She'd dusted her eyelids with smoky hues and had drawn a fine black line to skim her lower lashes. The make-up gave her a dramatic, dusky allure.

A disturbing fantasy flashed into living Technicolor in his head. He saw her in a different setting, somewhere remote, far away from this city, and she was leaning towards him, her dark eyelashes spiky and wet…her cheeks flushed, her pink lips softly parted…and her eyes were begging him to make love to her.

He cursed softly at his foolishness and spun on his heel, eager to move on, to find a quieter, less crowded bar. But he made the fatal mistake of glancing back over his shoulder.

And this time, he was touched more by her air of solitude than her beauty. Her gaze was fixed on a spot in the distance, and yet she was staring at it without interest, as if she was seeing something else, some inner turmoil.

He recognised that look. He knew the loneliness hovering like a shadowing hawk behind her lovely eyes. There were many times he'd felt that.

Tonight was one of them.

Each year, this anniversary became more and more difficult and he'd chosen to fly north to Cairns a few days earlier than his business commitments required, simply to avoid spending this particular night in Sydney.

He'd planned to spend the night alone—content to be a sightseer, wandering this sultry, tropical city at whim, hoping to blank out bad memories by renewing his acquaintance with the sights and sounds and smells of the far north. A solitary stranger in town.

But now he'd seen the girl at the bar.

And his plans had to change.

Alice was trying to be brave.

It wasn't easy to sit alone in a bar on her thirtieth birthday. Alone, for heaven's sake! She had a right to feel down. Seriously down.

The annoying thing was that she had no one but herself to blame; she'd run away from her birthday party. Not the party her workmates had wanted to throw, but the family gathering her mother had insisted on arranging.

Very early in the night, Aunt Bettina had voiced the family's collective thoughts.

'Poor Alice,' she'd said, her voice choking, while her eyes became moons of sympathy. 'Married before twenty and divorced before thirty. It's a crying shame.'

No one—repeat, no one—not a single member of the Madigan family had ever been divorced. Louisa, the family's genealogy expert, had researched on the Internet, so she was certain of this.

No one had been infertile either. And if the men in Alice's family had ever indulged in extramarital affairs, their women kept very quiet about it. It was an unspoken family law that Madigan women hung on to their husbands.

Alice had committed all three crimes—infertility, an unfaithful husband and a divorce. She was the family failure.

She'd been trying hard to feel good about herself in spite of these disasters. She'd survived a wrecked marriage with her ego intact—*just*. She knew that she was better alone than she'd ever been with Todd. And she'd learned the bitter lesson that a woman shouldn't rely on others—certainly not a husband or babies—to make her happy or to give meaning to her life.

It was up to her.

She'd come a long way in the past six months. But tonight her family made her feel like an obliterated body in a single-vehicle crash. No hope. Dead on arrival.

As if turning thirty wasn't a miserable enough milestone in any woman's life. As celebrations went, her party had been a flop.

And as soon as the cake was cut she'd made her excuses, claiming that her workmates, who hung out at the Hippo Bar on Friday nights, were waiting for her.

The only problem was that her friends weren't expecting her and by the time she arrived they'd moved on to a nightclub somewhere, and Alice didn't have the heart to track them all over town on their cellphones.

So here she was. On the night of her big Three-O. Looking down the barrel of the rest of her life. Alone.

'Another one?'

Alice blinked at the barman and he pointed to her empty glass. 'Did you enjoy the French Kiss?'

'Yes, it was delicious.'

'So you want to try another cocktail?'

Should she have another? Why not? This wasn't a night for being careful. Picking up the menu, she scanned the list of outrageous names and smiled. 'I think I'll be adventurous and go for a Screaming Orgasm this time.'

'And I'll have one, too,' said a lazy voice beside her.

Alice spun to her left and was surprised to find a man sitting on the stool right next to her. When had he arrived?

He smiled. Slowly. It was a smile that started at his eyes—light blue, clever and good-humoured—and took its time reaching his mouth. With the same lack of haste he let his gaze linger on her and he didn't try to hide the fact that he liked what he saw.

Something about his eyes and the very male way he was checking her out made her stomach feel ridiculously weightless—as if she'd suddenly toppled over the edge of a cliff.

'Hi,' the stranger said.

Alice had no experience of meeting men in bars; her ex-husband had been her first boyfriend and she'd married him before she was out of her teens. If only she could think of some smart, metro-chick response.

'Hi, yourself,' she replied.

At a guess, he was in his mid-thirties. He had dark brown hair with just the faintest hint of silver at the temples and a longish face. A strong face. He was lean and suntanned and dressed in chinos and an open-necked white shirt with long sleeves rolled back.

'You seem to be drinking alone,' he said. 'It's not a healthy habit.'

Alice felt compelled to defend herself. 'It's not actually a habit. This is a one-off experience.'

He accepted this with a slight nod. 'Are you having fun?'

'The best.' She straightened her shoulders. 'What about you?'

'I prefer the company of others.'

'But you're on your own tonight.'

'Ah, yes,' he admitted and he sent her another slow smile. 'But then, I have an excellent excuse.'

She drew a deep breath, aware that a kind of game had begun and the ball was in her court. 'You just got out of jail?'

His eyes widened slightly and then he chuckled. 'In a manner of speaking. I've escaped from Sydney. I only arrived in town today and I don't know anyone.' His blue gaze held hers for breathtaking seconds. 'Yet.'

OK. *Now* was the point when she should give this guy the brush-off. But their drinks arrived. And before she could pay, her neighbour pushed several bills across the bar.

'My shout,' he said.

She was about to protest.

But she changed her mind. Why the heck shouldn't she test her wings on a little light flirtation? She was thirty—and for the first time in her adult life she was out on the town as a free agent; two good reasons to let a rather nice-looking guy chat her up in a bar.

If he wanted to.

And if she decided she wanted to let him.

'So, what's your excuse for drinking alone?' he asked her.

'Aliens abducted my friends.'

One dark eyebrow lifted. 'How unfortunate for them.'

'Yes. I guess they'll wake up in the morning with their memories wiped clean.'

He grinned. 'It's happened to a few of my mates after a night on the town.'

Picking up her drink, Alice took a slow sip. 'What do you think of the cocktail?' She tried to feel detached as she watched the movements of his lips while he tasted his drink.

'Not bad.'

'Have you had one of these before?'

'No.' He held his glass to the light and gave the contents a swirl before taking a longer sip. And then he flashed her a wicked smile. 'This is my very first Orgasm.'

She almost choked, gasped for breath. A cloud of steam rose through her and she tried to ignore it. *Stay cool, Alice.* Lifting her glass, she offered him a shaky salute. 'Don't drink too fast, then.'

And just as she wondered if she was getting out of her depth, she was rescued by a voice calling from across the bar.

'Hey, Alice—happy birthday!'

It was a guy who worked in the same building as she did. He must have seen the banner the girls had strung in the foyer this morning. She didn't know him very well, so she gave him a quick wave and hoped he wouldn't come over. The conversation with this stranger was bordering on crazy, but she didn't want to be interrupted. Maybe it was the cocktails, but she was feeling a weird but wonderful sense of connection with him.

'Happy birthday, Alice?' the stranger asked, and he frowned sharply. 'Is it really your birthday?'

Oh, man. He looked upset. Was it because he'd realised she was a dead-set loser, abandoned by everyone on her birthday? She'd been hoping to come across as a very together urban goddess.

'I have a thing about birthdays,' she said, quickly. 'I never celebrate them. What are birthdays, after all? Here today, gone tomorrow. I mean, why make a big fuss about turning—*oops!*'

'Fair enough,' he said more equably. 'Although I've always thought that turning *oops* was something of a milestone.' Again his eyes held hers and they twinkled with such obvious amusement that she fancied she must have imagined that earlier frown.

'There's something to be said for making the most of any reason to celebrate,' he added.

She raised her glass. 'I'm celebrating.' But she didn't drink. She suspected she'd already had enough and set the glass down again. 'This conversation is getting a little lopsided.' She needed to change the subject before she got herself into trouble. 'You already know my name and my date of birth and I don't know the first thing about you.'

'What would you like to know?'

Are you married? He wasn't wearing a ring but that didn't mean a darn thing. 'Your name?'

'Liam. And if you're worried about an equal exchange of information, I'm thirty-six, or perhaps I should say oops plus six,' he added with a smile. 'And…' He paused.

'And?' She tried unsuccessfully to keep the curiosity out of her voice.

'It's my birthday today, too.'

'You're joking.'

'Not at all.' He pulled a wallet from his back trouser pocket and flipped it open on the bar. And there was his driver's licence. Conway, Liam Cooper. And sure enough, his date of birth was the fifth of September.

Alice frowned suddenly. Liam Cooper Conway. Where had she heard that name? Liam Conway. Mr Conway. Dr Conway. Professor Conway. *Inspector* Conway?

No…she was dreaming. She'd never met him before. Besides, he said he was from Sydney. He had a New South Wales driver's licence and he'd already told her he'd just arrived in town.

'Anything else you'd like to know?' he asked.

She thought about this and was only a little shocked to realise this meeting might lose its gloss if she learned too much about this man. She shook her head. Right now Liam Conway was an intriguing Man of Mystery, a figure of limitless potential. He could be anything…

What seemed more important than boring details like his occupation was the fact that he shared her birthday! Her star sign. My God, they were almost soul mates. She rewarded him with her warmest smile. 'Happy birthday, Liam Conway.'

'Thank you.' He returned his wallet to his pocket and lifted his glass. 'Are you going to finish your drink?'

'I'm not sure that I should.' She gave her cocktail a stir with her straw. 'I don't know what they put in these things.'

'Hmm…the ingredients of a Screaming Orgasm. That's a big question.'

This time, when their gazes met, his eyes signalled a very direct, unambiguous message, a message so

dark and sensual that she was both alarmed and excited. Her heart picked up pace, sweat filmed her skin
and she felt a sensuous tug deep within her. Good
grief. She couldn't remember the last time she'd felt
like this.

Desperate to change the subject she asked, 'Where
were you on your sixth birthday?'

Liam blinked as if his brain had been in a completely different country and it seemed to take him
ages to compute her question. 'Um—I was on my
parents' orchard down on the Granite Belt.'

'So, while I was being born, you were stuffing
yourself with peaches and plums?'

'Possibly. Although I would have preferred ice
cream if it was on offer.'

'No party?'

'My parents didn't have much time for parties—
except on significant birthdays.'

For a moment he seemed lost in a cloud of darkness. He downed his drink quickly and then gave a
little shake as if to rid himself of a ghostly presence.
Alice had the distinct impression he was sorry he'd
told her so much.

'That's why I like to celebrate now,' he said but
the intensity in his voice was at odds with his words.

'I'm all for celebrating.' But then she remembered
that she'd had enough to drink, so her options for
celebrating in a bar were limited. Perhaps it was time
for her to leave.

She pictured herself hopping off her bar stool,
thanking Liam Conway for the cocktail and bidding
him farewell. In her mind's eye she saw herself walking out of the bar and calling a taxi to take her home.

Back at her Edge Hill flat, she would listen to one of her favourite Spanish-guitar CDs and drink a chaste cup of hot chocolate, and then she'd read a paperback novel until she fell asleep.

She knew exactly what she would do, what she *should* do. It was all very clear.

But she didn't move.

'It really is bad luck to have your friends abducted by aliens on your birthday,' Liam said quietly.

'Yeah,' Alice agreed with a rueful smile. 'I was hoping I'd finished my run of bad luck.' And immediately she regretted saying that. 'Sorry, you're looking for fun, not hard-luck stories.'

Liam shrugged. 'I wasn't looking for anything in particular. Until I saw you.'

His smile sent a delicious shiver right through her and she reached for her abandoned drink.

'It was a guy who put those shadows in your eyes, wasn't it?' Liam said.

She was too surprised to be cautious. 'Yes.'

'A rat?'

'A toad.' She might have smiled at that, but to her dismay the scene she'd tried so hard to forget leapt into her mind and her sorry state came tumbling out. 'I—I came home early one afternoon and found him in bed with another woman.'

Pressing a fist against her mouth, she struggled again with the horror of the memory.

Liam looked genuinely upset. 'Toad is too polite for a man like that. Some of us have a lot to answer for.'

His unexpected empathy seemed to open the floodgates on the feelings she'd been working so hard to hide. 'Maybe I shouldn't have been so surprised,' she found herself saying. 'I'd been picking up the tell-tale signs that Todd was straying. I just didn't want to believe it.'

Tears sprang to her eyes. Annoyed, she blinked and Liam picked up a paper serviette from the counter. 'Your mascara looks great,' he said. 'Don't ruin it.'

'Thanks.' She dabbed at her eyes, took a deep breath and released a shaky little laugh. 'You know, the thing that really upset me was that Todd added insult to injury by bringing this other woman into *our* bedroom.'

'So you were living with this guy?'

'He was my husband. I was married to the toad.' She twisted a corner of the serviette. 'He knew how much I loved that room. I'd taken such care choosing everything—the curtains, the carpet, the bed linen. The dressing table came from my grandparents' place. They'd had it in their bedroom for their whole married life.' Looking up, she said, 'Sorry, I don't expect you to understand.'

Liam shook his head. 'But I do understand. He didn't just deceive you, he violated your special place.'

Liam Conway wasn't just gorgeous; he was sensitive, too. She'd almost forgotten such men existed.

'I hope you got rid of him,' he said.

'Absolutely, especially when I found that this woman was one of many.' She sighed. 'Our divorce came through four months ago.' And then she winced. Admitting her failed marriage always made her feel such a loser.

'No wonder you still look a little shell-shocked.'

'I'm fine now. Honestly. It's in the past.' The confession was off her chest and that was good, but she didn't want to bore this lovely man witless. 'I've got a new life ahead of me.'

'Another thing to celebrate,' he said. And then, 'So…why don't we go and find a place where we can dance?'

Heavens, she hadn't been dancing in years. Todd had always claimed he hated it, so they'd never danced, and she was way out of practice. 'I'm afraid I'm not much of a dancer,' she said.

'I don't believe that.' Liam stood and he was even taller than she'd expected. 'Come on,' he coaxed. 'It's our birthday. Let's kick up our heels.'

Kick up her heels? She sent a flustered glance towards her feet. Her strappy black sandals had rather high heels and she'd painted her toenails bright berry-red to match her red and black floral dress.

From above her she heard Liam say, 'They look like dancing feet to me.'

She took a deep breath and looked up at him again. *Gulp.* There was something so compelling about him, something unmistakably masculine about the contained strength in his lean body and in the strong, straight planes of his face, in the intention signalled by his eyes. She should make a quick get-away now, before she became completely entranced.

She didn't want to get involved with another man, not yet, when the war-wounds from her divorce were still raw.

But a voice inside her was urging her to throw caution to the winds.

His eyes are as soulful as they are sexy. Why hes-

*itate? It's only dancing, after all. And anyway, surely
you have the perfect excuse to be daring? You'll
never have another thirtieth birthday.*

She picked up her bag from the bar.

Go on, Alice. He seems s-o-o-o nice.

She flashed him a bright return smile. 'OK.
Dancing sounds like fun.'

He grinned. 'Let's go.'

Outside on the footpath a photographer was taking
a photo of a trio of laughing girls and, as Alice and
Liam passed, there was a blinding flash from the cam-
era.

The photographer called after them, 'Sir, can I take
a photo of you and your lovely lady?'

Liam scowled and waved him away.

'Welcome to North Queensland,' said Alice. 'The
local papers are always snapping people for their social pages.'

'Glad we escaped, then.' Liam took her hand.

Oh, heavens. She was super-sensitive to every mil-
limetre of his skin, to the supple strength of his fingers
interlaced with hers.

'Where's the best place in town for dancing?' he
asked.

'The Reef Club is supposed to be very good.'

'Supposed?'

'I've never actually been there.'

He shot her a curious glance and she hoped it
wasn't because he could feel the wave of warmth that
had swept through her when he touched her.

More than likely he was wondering about her re-
stricted social life. If he asked, she would be prepared
to explain that, although she worked for a tourist com-

pany, she specialised in regional tours and she didn't have much personal experience of local night spots.

Liam didn't ask. And Alice was relieved, because an explanation would have led to more details about her failed marriage. Todd had preferred to spend his weekends on game-fishing trips out to the Barrier Reef, or heavy drinking and gambling with his mates, rather than taking her out on the town.

But telling Liam about that could be an information overload. There was every chance he didn't really want to know much about her at all.

He simply wanted her company for an hour or so. No strings attached. And that suited Alice just fine. The last thing she wanted was to leap straight from her disastrous marriage into another relationship. Besides, she'd always supposed that divorcees indulged in this kind of throwing-off-the-shackles adventure.

But she would feel a darned sight calmer about going dancing with a man she'd just met if she didn't feel quite so attracted to him. She hadn't expected to feel so quickly attuned, to be so instantly captivated and breathless.

It was more than a decade since she'd first fallen for the best-looking footballer in her high school. She knew she was out of practice at the whole guy-girl scenario, but surely she shouldn't feel such an emotional connection with a stranger? Or such a heady jolt of awareness whenever Liam Conway looked at her? Whenever she looked at him?

How on earth would she cope when they started dancing? Perhaps she should start praying now. With luck, the band at the Reef Club played loud, fast music where dancers more or less jigged around without touching.

No such luck.

One step into the foyer of the Reef Club and she saw that the lighting was low, the music slow and bluesy, and the dance floor dark and crowded. One look at the dangerous smoulder in Liam Conway's blue eyes and she knew she was in trouble.

Liam sent her a slow smile. 'Shall we dance, birthday girl?' And without even waiting for her reply, he took her hand and led her onto the shadowy dance floor. And suddenly it was happening. Alice was in his arms.

She was excited, terrified—electrified, her senses on full alert. Cocooned by the darkness and the sexy croon of a saxophone, they swayed together slowly and she felt everything super-keenly—the touch of Liam's breath softly stirring her hair, the muscled strength of his shoulder beneath her hand, his taut, lean body brushing tantalisingly close to hers.

If she closed her eyes her nostrils filled with the subtle tang of his aftershave, and if she opened them again she was captivated by the lazy sweep of the strobe light, giving her glimpses of Liam's face and the contrast between her pale skin and his tan.

From the moment she'd met this man she'd been walking a tightrope. Perhaps her emotions were tipping her off balance? She felt spellbound by him— by their coinciding birthdays, by the kind way he'd listened to her sob story, by the hungry way he looked at her. And now, in his arms, she was incredibly ablaze.

Clearly the long months of loneliness during her separation and divorce had taken their toll.

She wanted Liam to kiss her. She wanted his hands on her body, and yes, she wanted him to make love to her.

The wanting filled her head, blanking out reason.

And she suspected that Liam's mind was on the same fast-track. Despite the ease with which he moved about the dance floor, there was no mistaking the subtle tension in his body, or the unsubtle desire in his eyes.

His lips brushed her forehead and a soft, almost desperate little sigh escaped him.

The dark, masculine sound plunged deep within Alice and the last, fragile threads of her resistance gave way. Helpless, she melted against him and desire flowered, surged and spilled inside her.

He drew her even closer, and nudged against her with sweet, unbearable precision. With his mouth against her ear, he murmured, 'Have you any idea how bloody beautiful you are?'

They were hardly the words or the actions of a gentleman and she knew she should have been shocked. But she was too lost inside her cloud of desire. And her throat was so choked with emotion she couldn't have voiced a protest even if she'd tried to.

And then, in the lull between one song and the next, he said, 'Birthday girl, I want to take you home.'

Oh, God. Alice buried her face in his shoulder, her heart beating like a wild creature. She'd known from the moment she left the Hippo Bar that there was every possibility the evening was heading in this direction, but for one hot, terrifying moment of panic her courage failed her. A casual fling was so outside her experience.

Liam gently stroked her neck. 'Bad idea?'

Was it? Alice tried to think calmly, but she was such a swirling mass of emotion and desire she was beyond the point of rational decision-making.

But she knew there was one important question she had to ask. She tilted her face so that her husky whisper reached him. 'Tell me one thing; are you married?'

'No.' He said that so definitely she knew that he spoke the truth.

Raising her eyes to meet the hot intensity of his, she said, 'It's not a bad idea, Liam.'

The rasp of his indrawn breath made her shiver. He was as tense, as consumed as she was. She could hardly breathe.

They left the Reef Club holding hands and yet hardly daring to look at each other as they passed beneath the glow of overhead lights.

'I didn't bring my car,' Alice said. 'Did you?'

For the briefest moment she sensed a different kind of tension in him. 'No; I haven't organised a vehicle yet.'

'Well,' she said lightly, 'there should be plenty of taxis around tonight.'

She felt impossibly shy as they stood near the edge of the footpath, waiting for a taxi. 'I—I guess this is where one of us says, your place or mine?'

His light blue eyes seemed to shimmer. 'I'm sure that should be your choice.'

The taxi arrived and they slipped into the back seat.

Liam glanced at Alice as the driver waited expectantly. This was it; no turning back now. And it was her choice.

She gave the driver the address of her flat in Edge Hill. Better to be on home ground. The thought gave her an illusion of control. Besides, she was rather proud of her flat; she'd bought it with her share from the sale of the house she'd shared with Todd.

It was ultra-modern and brand new and it was such a novelty to have her very own private space that she kept it looking fabulous. Her friends teased her that she was expecting *Home Beautiful* magazine to call, begging to feature her place in their next big spread.

Thinking about her friends' gentle teasing helped to calm her as the taxi sped them through the dark streets. It helped too that Liam sat a little apart from her and she was relieved that he wasn't panting all over her on the back seat.

Nevertheless she could sense his tension and her body burned with breathless, coiling anticipation. What kind of lover was this man?

What kind of lover was she? Not much of one, if Todd's straying from her bed was any indication. But there was something about Liam's frank and open appreciation of her that shored up the confidence Todd had undermined.

A welcome cool breeze greeted them as they stepped from the taxi. Above them a new moon spilled a romantic silver sheen over the lush fronds of the palm trees that lined Alice's street.

'Nice location,' Liam said and then he fell silent as they walked along the brick path flanked by newly landscaped gardens.

It wasn't till Alice was fishing in her bag for her door key that she was hit by a rush of sudden doubts. Was she making a terribly stupid mistake? She didn't know anything about this man. She didn't do this kind of thing.

If a clairvoyant had told her she would bring home a good-looking stranger from a bar, she would have laughed in her face and demanded her money back.

When it came to dating trends, Alice had been left behind in the last century. Although her unattached friends seemed to think nothing of having sex for no other reason than because they fancied a guy, until tonight Alice had never dreamed of being so rash. Not in her wildest fantasies. Well, OK, maybe in her *wildest* fantasies—but since when were they reliable?

Perhaps she should suggest coffee. She had a lovely new espresso machine and she could take Liam Conway into her shiny, trendy kitchen and make coffee and insist that they talk some more. She could get him to talk about himself. There were so many things she should know before they—

Too late. Liam reached for her as soon as the front door closed behind them. And thoughts of coffee and the questions that had seemed so important scampered clear out of her head as he drew her in to him. And his lips met hers.

Oh... His lips were soft and firm and warm and super-slow. Alice's legs almost buckled beneath her.

'You have the most gorgeous mouth,' he murmured.

'I'm...rather taken with yours.' She was a little stunned to hear how sinking-out-of-control she sounded.

And then he touched his lips to the side of her throat. 'And you have the most kissable neck.'

Ah, yes. Flattery and sensuous, lazy lips were a heart-stopping combination. So different from Todd.

No, she wasn't going to think about Todd. Just Liam. Just this—his mesmerising lips exploring her skin, making her body warm and wanton. She knew now that she'd been starving for intimate contact.

A hot, honeyed languor seemed to fill her. In a dazzle of warmth, she pressed her thighs and hips against Liam's and arched her neck, silently begging him for more kisses.

Liam obliged. While his hands wedged her body hard against his, his mouth traced a sensuous path down her neck, into the little valley at her collar-bone and then up again. He kissed her ear lobe.

'Best ears in the southern hemisphere,' he said and he teased her ear with the tip of his tongue, and she was overtaken by a desperate need to nibble-kiss the rough skin all the way along his jaw.

His response was a sexy choked groan and the next moment he scooped her up in his arms. 'Which way?' he murmured as her feet left the floor.

Without a beat of hesitation she pointed down the hallway to her bedroom.

CHAPTER TWO

IT FELT a little crazy to wake next morning with Liam Conway in her bed. Crazy and wonderful. And just a bit sad. This was going to be the hard part—the morning after the night before.

She and Liam could hardly pretend to be strangers after a night of amazing, heaven-on-earth passion, but just the same, the deeper getting-to-know-you stuff that they'd skipped wasn't going to happen now. Soon Liam would be leaving, walking out of her life, and Alice would have to put on a brave face and remember that she didn't mind; it was what she wanted.

Besides, now that she knew she was infertile, casual dating was probably all men would want from her.

With her head propped on her hand, she lay on her side and watched Liam wake, his eyes blinking, showing her snippets of blue like glimpses of morning sky.

He saw that she was watching him, and he smiled at her. 'Good morning.'

'Morning.'

His eyes were drinking her in now and he reached to touch her hair as it tumbled about her shoulders. Did she look a mess? Or like a woman who'd enjoyed a night of blissful ravishment? There was something about broad daylight that was so, well, revealing.

Liam, of course, looked better than ever. The darkening shadow on his jaw gave him a trendy, designer-stubble sexiness, and his bulky shoulders were bronzed, almost glowing, an effect no doubt enhanced by the sunshine filtering through the filmy bedroom curtains.

Not that she should be lying here ogling him. Her job this morning was to facilitate his farewell—a friendly but matter-of-fact exit.

'It's going to be a nice day,' she said and immediately winced. Not a clever start. She sounded like a tour guide setting off with a group of holidaymakers for the Great Barrier Reef. But what was she supposed to say? *Thanks for the most amazing, beautiful, emotionally moving, best sex of my life?*

It was the absolute truth. But would Liam believe her? She'd travelled to the stars last night, but for all she knew their lovemaking might have been everyday-average for him.

He stretched and, with his hands stacked beneath his head, he glanced where she'd been looking, at the window and the branches of palm trees against the patch of blue sky. 'Another day in paradise, as the tourist brochures say.' He switched his gaze back to her and smiled lazily. 'And you and I are another day older.'

Indeed. Their birthdays were a thing of the past. Here today, gone tomorrow.

Alice sat up, holding the sheet around her. 'I'm glad you stayed the night,' she said shyly. 'I would have felt a bit cheap if you'd left as soon as we'd finished—um—celebrating.'

Liam frowned. 'It would be a crime to make you

feel cheap. You're a very special woman, Alice.' The creases in his brow melted as his frown morphed into a smile. 'And as I remember it, we spent most of the night celebrating.'

Alice felt herself blush. Then the rest of her began to warm up as Liam continued to look at her. And look.

Oh, heavens. The daylight made no difference. She was as susceptible to him now as she had been in the night.

She wished she was savvier about how these things worked. Where did a one-night stand end and the beginning of a relationship start?

She wasn't looking for a relationship, couldn't bear to leave herself vulnerable, only to be hurt again.

'I—I'll make some coffee,' she said, edging away. 'Or perhaps you'd prefer tea?'

If Liam was surprised by her withdrawal he made a quick recovery. 'Coffee would be fantastic.'

She drew a deep breath of relief. She'd half expected him to drag her into his arms and she knew she would have been too weak to resist. But fortunately, he accepted her decision with good grace. When she wriggled towards the edge of the bed, he didn't try to stop her.

She headed for the bathroom and, once she'd finished there, she wrapped herself inside a white towelling bath robe and went through to the kitchen to start the coffee. It wasn't long before Liam joined her, showered, but still unshaven, and dressed in the clothes he'd worn last night.

The sight of him strolling into her kitchen was enough to make her heart do a somersault. Darn. Here she was, safely surrounded by pots and pans, and Liam Conway had the same disturbing effect on her as he did on the dance floor or in her bedroom.

'That coffee smells sensational,' he said.

She held up a packet she'd taken from the freezer. 'Would you like croissants?'

'Is that what you're having?'

She nodded. 'It's my Saturday-morning treat. Croissants and coffee and the weekend papers out on the deck.' She fingered the lapels of her bathrobe. 'I wasn't going to bother with the papers this morning, but if you want them it's not far to the shop. You can grab them while I warm these croissants.'

He thought about this for a moment and then shook his head. 'I can do without news from the outside world today. I don't officially start work here till Monday. There's time enough then to come to grips with what's going on.'

'So you've actually moved to Cairns to start a new job?' She tried not to sound particularly interested and she ducked her face as she slipped the croissants into the oven.

'I've bought a new business that has a branch here,' he said in an offhand way that suggested he didn't want to go into details. 'This is a great place by the way.'

'Thank you.'

'I take it that green is your favourite colour?'

He was looking at her collection of green crockery and glassware which she kept on display on open shelving.

'I guess it must be.' She smiled, pleased that he'd

noticed them. 'Virgos are supposed to like white best.'

'Are we?'

'According to the experts. But I've been collecting green bits and pieces since I was about twelve. It started with a plate shaped like a water-lily pad and went on from there.' She shrugged. 'It's become a minor obsession.'

Todd had hated her green collection. 'We're not Irish,' he'd yelled at her and in one of his bad moods he'd smashed her favourite piece. For the past five years she'd kept the collection locked away. Now it was free again.

Liam picked up a green and white bowl fashioned like a field of clover with delicately scalloped edges, and he turned it over and examined the maker's name on the base. 'This is great. It has personality and it sure beats the plain white minimalist stuff you get in restaurants.' He set it back carefully.

As she selected napkins from an overhead cupboard, she framed a question in her head about his new business, but she hesitated to ask because he could have already told her if he'd wanted to. But then she decided to dive in anyway.

'What business have you bought?'

'A travel company.'

No. Alice stiffened and felt cold all over. She stared at him. 'Which travel company?'

He stared back at her, warily, without answering.

'Please tell me you haven't bought Kanga Tours?'

A muscle in his jaw jerked and he continued to frown at her as he very deliberately straightened his shoulders and folded his arms over his chest. 'Would it matter if I had?'

'No…well, yes—it would.'

'I beg your pardon?'

She felt a slam of panic. 'I can't believe this.'

'Can't believe what?' His eyes narrowed and, if it were possible, his expression was even more cautious. 'Why? What's the problem?'

She switched her gaze to the glass-fronted door of her oven. The croissants were already turning golden.

'What do you know about Kanga Tours?' Liam demanded. 'I had the company checked out thoroughly. I got the best advice. I know the growth in the north hasn't been as strong as expected, but that's why I'm here. To turn it around. I believe in hands-on management. Overall the company seemed to be a damn good business proposition.'

'Oh, it's a good business,' she said while her heart hammered. 'If you're a good manager, you'll make plenty of money here.'

'So, why are you looking like it's really bad news?'

She bit her lip. He wasn't going to like this.

'For God's sake, Alice. You look like I confessed I was a terrorist.'

'I—I work there. At Kanga Tours.'

His jaw dropped. Fast. He stared at her and, as her words really sank in, he glanced away sharply. Cursing, he raked angry fingers through his hair.

Alice knew what he was thinking—that if word leaked out that the new boss had slept with one of the staff on his very first night in town, there could be all sorts of unpleasant ramifications. He could be branded as a sleaze, a predator, and she would be the tart, the wild divorcee, sleeping her way into the new boss's favour.

Office affairs made ripples that very often became waves, waves that could swamp the boat. It could be just awful. For both of them.

She remembered the stir among the staff last week when Dennis Ericson first told them that a new boss was arriving from Sydney.

And then she was struck by a light-bulb moment. 'Conway! For heaven's sake. Now I remember why your name sounded familiar last night.' Clasping her hands to the sides of her face, she let out a groan. 'If only I'd thought of it earlier, but I didn't make the connection. When I went to the Hippo Bar the last thing on my mind was my work or a new boss.'

'Quite.'

The single, carefully clipped monosyllable seemed to cut through her. Neither she nor Liam had been thinking about work last night. They'd been totally distracted. Just thinking about how very distracted they'd been made her blush.

The oven pinged and she was grateful for a different kind of distraction. Shoving her hands into padded gloves, she pulled the croissants from the oven and avoided Liam's gaze as she popped them onto the plates she'd already set on a tray, along with the coffee and cutlery and a pot of strawberry jam.

In one bound Liam was across the room and taking the tray from her. 'Let me carry that.'

'Thanks.' At least he wasn't so angry that he forgot his manners.

Their hands brushed as Alice handed him the tray and she made the mistake of looking up. His eyes were so close to her now. Too close. A look passed between them, a look that spoke of intimate secrets, of everything they'd shared last night—of Liam's caresses, his whispered endearments, and her wild response to the satiny heat of him thrusting deep inside her.

It had been bad enough trying to carry on at work through the mess of the divorce. But how could she cope now, while her boss was a walking reminder of more things she needed to forget? The memories of their intimacy would stay with her. Every day.

A mask seemed to slip over Liam's features and he turned to carry their breakfast things onto her back deck, which was cleverly designed to give privacy while offering a view of the tropical courtyard below. For the next few minutes their conversation was confined to the coffee and croissants and whether Liam would like milk or sugar or jam. But Alice was bursting with the need to talk about their predicament.

'We were supposed to be going our separate ways this morning,' she said.

He sent her a sharp, searching look. 'Is that what you wanted?'

Her heart gave a startled leap. 'Well, yes, of course. It's what you wanted, too.' The stern expression in his eyes prompted her to add, 'Isn't it?'

To her dismay he didn't answer. Instead, he took another sip of coffee and put the cup down slowly. 'Let's sort this work issue out. What's your role at Kanga Tours?'

He was changing the subject. Why? Was he upset with her? Had she read him incorrectly? Surely he hadn't hoped for more than last night?

The thought that Liam might have wanted to continue their relationship set Alice suddenly adrift, swept away without warning by a flash flood. She struggled to remember his question.

'I—I'm one of the specialist consultants,' she said at last. 'I look after the customers who want specialised tours in tune with particular interests.'

Liam nodded. 'Do you cover everything? The reef, the rainforest and the outback?'

'Sure.' Pride set her chin at a tilt. 'Everything from snorkelling or diving on the reef, to night-time spotlighting in the rainforest and outback cattle musters. They want it, I package it for them—even speciality restaurant tours.'

A smile pulled at the corner of his mouth. 'I'm sure you're very good at it.'

'I really enjoy my job. Since my divorce it's been my life saver.'

He didn't respond immediately.

'Look,' she said. 'I know it's going to be awkward for you to have me at work, but I won't let on that I—I've met you. I can be discreet and professional.'

'Yes, you're a bright girl.'

A bright girl. It was rather a comedown from a very special woman, which was what he'd called her half an hour ago.

'I think that's the best way to play it,' he said as his long fingers broke off a piece of croissant. 'From now on our relationship will be entirely professional.'

'Yes.'

'There's no need to compromise either of us. We're mature adults. We can give each other space and get on with our jobs.'

'Yes,' she agreed again. 'There are at least ten employees at Kanga Tours, so we won't be falling all over each other.'

But…there would be almost daily contact.

'I imagine I'll be out of the office a great deal,' Liam added, as if he was reading her mind. 'Especially at first. There's a lot to do to ensure the company's viability, so I'll be out and about. I want to find new premises.'

'So our old building in the backstreets isn't good enough for…?' Alice saw the warning spark in Liam's eyes and broke off in mid-sentence.

'I need a prime location,' he said crisply. 'Something where all the action is—on the Esplanade with mountain and ocean views perhaps, right on the tourist and backpacker thoroughfare.'

She drained her coffee-cup. 'I'm sure you'll want to put your own stamp on the company.'

He didn't answer. He helped himself to the strawberry jam and then ate his croissant slowly and seemed to pay close attention to a cluster of Golden Cane palms in the courtyard beneath them.

When he finished, he said, 'Thanks, Alice, that was excellent, but now I should leave you to get on with your weekend.'

She forced a smile and hoped it was broad enough to give the impression that she had so many exciting things lined up for this weekend she didn't know where to start.

Liam began to gather up their breakfast things. 'Leave them,' she insisted. After all, she had two whole days to carry them inside and wash them.

What else was she going to do?

Weekends had always come as a bonus at the end of a busy working week, but suddenly this one loomed emptily before her. She was already focusing on Monday morning, and seeing Liam again. But she was worried too. Darn it. Why did he have to be her boss?

'Would you like me to call a taxi?' she offered.

'No, thanks, I'll walk. It's a great morning for having a look around and getting to know my new home-town.'

Her bare feet padded on the timber floor and she knotted her bathrobe more tightly at the waist as she followed him to her front door. A lump jammed her throat as he opened the door and turned to her.

Oh, heavens, last night had been so wonderful. The most beautiful night ever. It made up for all the hurt…

She suddenly wanted to cry. Crazy! No. She mustn't.

But what should she do now? Kiss Liam on the cheek? Wave him goodbye?

She forced another smile and held out her hand. 'See you at the office, Mr Conway.'

'Alice, don't.' Dark colour stained his face as he clasped her hand. 'Don't be like that.'

Like what? she wanted to ask.

But he was staring at her hand in his. And then suddenly his shoulder nudged the door closed again and, to her amazement, he pulled her roughly to him and his mouth came down hard on hers.

The passionate force of his kiss stunned her. Backing against the door, he pulled her to him, his mouth possessive, uncompromising, bruising. Her heart pounded in answer. Her body softened in instant surrender.

After just one night the smell and the taste and the feel of him were wonderfully familiar. A sweet sense of recognition overwhelmed her—the strong feeling that she belonged in these arms, with this man. She was tinder to his fire, ablaze at the first contact.

Her lips welcomed him. Her hands hungrily explored the muscly wonder of his shoulders; they twined in his hair. Her breasts strained for his touch.

And then, too soon, way too soon, he lifted his head and set her a little apart from him. His eyes glittered with an unreadable emotion.

'Damn,' he said, making the word sound both soft and harsh at once. 'That wasn't the way I'd planned to say goodbye.' He touched his lips gently to her forehead. 'I'm sorry, Alice. It won't happen again. From now on I'll be on my best behaviour.'

Too overcome and breathless to answer, she pressed her fingers to her lips to hold back a protest. Once more he opened the door and this time he stepped outside. He sent her one brief, scorching glance, and then he turned and strode swiftly away without looking back.

She watched him go with her fingers still pressed against her lips. Lips that were tender from the imprint of his kiss.

CHAPTER THREE

LIAM spent most of the weekend at the office, working his way through the company's files and planning his business strategies. He was determined to lift the Cairns branch's performance to match what he'd recently achieved in Sydney. As a self-made man, he'd worked impossibly hard over the past decade and he'd developed his own formula for revitalising a business.

New premises and a big investment in promotion and marketing were high on his agenda. And a staff performance appraisal. Several years ago he'd been forced to replace many of the inherited staff with a new team.

Could he do that again?

What about Alice? God help him. Could he be hard-headed and impartial enough to sack her if it was necessary?

All weekend his mind was constantly flooded by memories of her, of her heart-stopping, gut-wrenching loveliness, of the way she'd looked with her dark hair spread across the pillow, her rosy lips parted, inviting him to kiss her. She was so sweet and yet so wildly sensual. How could her husband ever have left her?

Liam had been consumed by an insane desire for her.

But office romances often led to trouble and trouble in business could reach atomic proportions. Staking a claim on Alice Madigan would place his goal, the success of his new business enterprise, in jeopardy. He couldn't take that risk, not when dark, insistent shadows from his past still haunted him.

He had a debt to pay, which left him with no choice but to put his business goals first. Always.

At the sound of a knock on his door on Monday morning Liam looked up to find Dennis Ericson, the branch office manager, lounging a casual hip against the door frame and wearing a supercilious smile.

'Good morning, Dennis.' Liam rose and held out his hand. The men had met before when Liam was making his pre-purchase investigations, but not as employer and employee. Dennis was in his mid-to-late forties, a family man, going thin on top and soft around the middle.

He accepted Liam's handshake, but the wry grimace on his face somewhat marred the sincerity of the gesture.

'You've settled in quickly, then,' he said, casting an openly curious glance around the office, checking the few small changes the new boss had made to its layout.

Liam nodded. 'Spent the weekend in here, going through files.'

The silly grin returned. 'And have you claimed your prize?'

'What prize?'

For answer, Dennis shot him a sideways, narrow-eyed glance.

Liam sensed that he was being set up. 'What are you talking about?'

'Saturday's *Cairns Post*,' Dennis said ominously. 'Page three.'

Liam shook his head. 'I didn't check the weekend papers. Is it something important? Some corporate offer?'

At that Dennis laughed. From his hip pocket he extracted what looked like a newspaper cutting and he flipped it onto the desk.

Annoyed by the smugness of the fellow, Liam refused to rise to the bait. He knew from experience that there was always someone wanting to get the upper hand with the new boss on the first day. He gave the folded cutting a cursory glance, and then stood very still and perfectly silent. Watching Dennis. Waiting.

Dennis's smile slipped. His Adam's apple slid up and down and, when Liam refused to move, he pouted. Finally, he picked up the clipping and unfolded it. 'Take a gander at this.'

Liam scanned it. Bloody hell.

'Aren't you lucky, sir? You're this week's Mystery Winner.' Dennis seemed to take pleasure from his boss's obvious surprise. His cockiness revived. 'Dinner for two at The Beach House,' he said. 'All you have to do is give the local newspaper office a call.'

It was a photo of Liam leaving the Hippo Bar. With Alice. Clipped and enlarged, no doubt, from a shot the photographer had taken of three girls whose faces were rather out of focus in the foreground. He and Alice looked blissfully happy. Intimate. They were holding hands and her head was dipping towards him as if she was listening intently to something he said.

A white ring circled his head and the caption above

the photo read: *Who is this man?* The text below explained, as Dennis had, that this mystery winner could claim his prize of a dinner for two.

'Do these mystery prizes happen often?' he asked.

'Every week,' replied Dennis smugly.

So much for keeping that night under wraps.

'Nice work, boss.' The edge to Dennis's voice was sharp enough to cut chain wire. 'I suppose we can skip the lecture on management probity and staff relations?'

Teeth gritted against a biting retort, Liam screwed the paper into a ball and tossed it across the office to the waste-paper basket. He was grateful that it curved in a perfect arc and fell neatly into the basket, dead centre. 'I know what you're thinking,' he said quietly.

'That you started getting extra-friendly with the staff the minute you hit town?'

Liam's response was to move past Dennis, to reach for the door and to close it with deliberate control.

'Sit down, Dennis.' With a curt nod he indicated the chair by the desk. 'You and I are going to have a little chat.'

Dennis sat. And his confident smirk began to wane as Liam took the high-backed leather executive chair and leaned back, watching him, without speaking.

Liam was damned if he was going to let this fellow launch a smear campaign. He knew that if he didn't act promptly, Alice's reputation would be dirt by morning-tea time.

With his elbow, he gave a file clearly marked *Dennis Ericson* a surreptitious nudge towards the front of his desk and then he stabbed at his desk phone for front of house reception.

'Sally,' he said, enjoying the way Dennis's eyes bulged when he read the name on the folder. 'Hold all my calls, please. And don't send anyone through to my office. It's most important that I'm not interrupted for the next twenty minutes.'

'Morning, Dennis.' Alice called her greeting as they passed in the hall outside her office.

'Morning,' he growled rudely, without making eye contact.

What was eating him?

Gulp. Had it started already? Was this because he'd seen the photo in the paper? The phone calls from her family had begun about five minutes after Liam left her on Saturday. Alice's mother and each of her aunts had rung, all demanding details about the strange man in the photo.

No one from work had contacted her, but she knew it was silly to hope that, by some miracle, none of them had seen the photo. She'd been dreading coming to the office this morning.

'What's the matter? I'm not late, am I?' She glanced at her watch. She *was* late, actually, thanks to traffic lights on the blink at a busy intersection, but not enough to upset anyone, especially as it was well-known that she often worked late or through her lunch hour without extra pay.

Dennis pursed his lips. 'I'm sure you can be as late as you like from now on.' He continued on, calling over his shoulder, 'You're sitting pretty now, Alice.'

Oh, great. That more or less confirmed her fears.

There was only one way to play it this morning. Cool. Carry on as if it was business as usual.

She went through to the office she shared with two other travel consultants, Mary-Ann and Shana.

'You know what's eating Dennis?' she asked. And then she realised that playing it cool was a good idea in theory…but the who's-she-trying-to-kid? look on her workmates' faces made her stomach pitch.

Mary-Ann clicked a button to boot up her computer. 'It's not so much a matter of *what's* eating Dennis, but *who*,' she said. 'Actually, it's who's eating him and spitting him out into little pieces.'

'And the answer is the new boss,' added Shana. 'First morning on the job and this Liam Conway's kicking heads. He lined poor Dennis up for a performance appraisal.'

'Oh.' Alice sat down quickly, a split-second before her legs began to shake.

'Instead of kicking heads he should pull his own head in,' muttered Shana.

'Don't tell me the new boss is an ogre?'

Shana rolled her eyes. 'As if we need to tell *you* anything about him. Why don't you tell us?'

Taking in her workmates' identical expressions, Alice released her breath with a soft sigh. 'OK, you've seen the photo in the *Post*.'

'Of course we've seen it.'

'How could we miss it?'

'But,' added Mary-Ann, 'we didn't know who the guy was till this morning.'

Shana came around to the front of her desk and crossed her arms over her chest. 'At least we know now why you weren't interested in the birthday party we offered to throw for you.'

Mary-Ann added her bit. 'I thought you were supposed to be at your mother's on Friday night.'

'I was,' said Alice. 'But it was awful and I left.'

'Hmm.' Mary-Ann looked momentarily sympathetic and then doubtful.

'Honest, guys. I went to the Hippo Bar to look for you, but you weren't there.'

'Ever hear of these little devices?' Shana waved her cell-phone. 'They're the latest means of communication. You can speed dial a friend at the touch of a button.'

'OK, OK.' Alice raised her hands to ward off their anger. 'Give me a break. Look, meeting Liam Conway was totally unexpected. He came into the bar. I was on my own and, well, we kinda clicked.' She took a quick breath. 'But it was a one-off thing. I won't be seeing him again.'

The girls were leaning towards her now, faces intent. It was clear they expected more.

'Clicked as in—totally clicked?' asked Mary-Ann.

Alice thought it best to ignore that query. 'I had no idea he was our new boss,' she said. 'And he didn't know me from Eve. It was a really weird coincidence. Bad luck.'

'Bad luck?' cried Shana. 'Honey, I'm not sure that's what you call it.'

'When it turns out he's my new boss, I do.'

'May I interrupt?'

The voice at the door startled them. There was a collective gasp and a surge of near-panic hit Alice as she turned to see Liam standing there.

Surely he must have heard their conversation?

He came into the room and she dropped her gaze,

dusted a crumb from her keyboard. This was going to be worse than she'd feared. One look at Liam and she was remembering the way those grim lips had been soft and hot on her body.

The girls were watching her. She couldn't be coy or self-conscious. This first encounter at work with Liam was the Big Test.

Taking another quick breath for control, she looked up again and managed a smile. 'Good morning.' She was aware of Shana sliding a watchful, sideways look in her direction. 'Have you met our other consultants, Mary-Ann Dayton—and Shana Holmes?'

Liam shook their hands, greeted them with easy smiles. And then he stood in the middle of the room with his hands resting lightly on his hips, nudging his suit jacket aside.

Clean-shaven, dark and good-looking and dressed in his business suit, he was every inch a corporate leader, dead set on going places.

His blue eyes skirted over Alice as he looked directly at Mary-Ann and then Shana. 'I know the photo in the *Cairns Post* has caused quite a stir and I'd like to set the record straight,' he said. 'I expect Alice has told you about our chance meeting in the bar last Friday evening.'

He waited, eyebrows raised expectantly. 'Right,' he continued, once he'd elicited nods of agreement from the girls. 'I'm here to assure you that there are no grounds for gossip. That photo means nothing and I don't expect to hear any more about it from anyone in this company.'

His cool, no-nonsense gaze flicked to Alice, causing considerable difficulty with her breathing. 'What's important from now on is this business,' he said, still looking straight at her. 'Your jobs.' His hands dropped from his hips.

Alice couldn't believe how awful this felt. Liam wasn't putting a foot wrong. He was doing everything he'd said he would and it was sensible to clear the air, to nip rumours in the bud. He was distancing himself from her, as he'd promised, turning from her lover into her boss.

She should be pleased. She *was* pleased. In her head.

But her heart felt like a heavy stone, sinking… sinking…

'OK,' Liam said. 'Let's move on to more important matters. I'd like to schedule a full staff meeting for tomorrow.'

'Alice, can you come through to my office?'

Liam held his breath. There was an unsettling pause before she replied.

'I'm sorry, Mr Conway, I'm busy with clients at the moment. Can you give me—oh, say, fifteen minutes?'

'Certainly.' Liam swallowed. He'd seen little of her over the past week—just the occasional glimpse from a distance down the corridor. Now the sound of her voice triggered a constriction in his throat.

He knew he'd been avoiding her. Cowardly of him? No doubt. Untenable for an effective working environment? Most certainly.

'Come as soon as you're free,' he said.

She wasn't free for another forty-five minutes and he distracted himself by making phone calls, continuing to contact the various resorts and attractions the company dealt with. He was questioning the people who ran them to find out what his staff and consultants were doing well and what they were doing wrong.

When at last Alice knocked on his door, he jumped to his feet. 'You've had a busy morning,' he said.

'Yes.'

'No problems? Nothing I should know about?'

'No, just some complicated transport arrangements for a Japanese group.'

Something about the way she said that made him wonder if her delay had been deliberate. Was she trying to avoid him as carefully as he'd been avoiding her? 'Please, take a seat.'

She sat very primly, shoulders back, ankles crossed neatly. She was wearing a short grey skirt and now she made an attempt to camouflage its hemline by positioning a notebook and a pen just so.

But the skirt wasn't the only problem. The pale, intensely feminine blouse beneath her businesslike jacket was damnably distracting. The blouse wasn't transparent, but the way his imagination worked it might as well have been.

Liam wondered if he should insist that his staff wear an ultra-conservative uniform. Then again, that wouldn't be much use. It was Alice who was distracting, not her choice of clothes.

She looked demure, almost prim, here in his office, but all he could think of was how uninhibited she'd been when she was alone with him, how passionately she'd made love.

He snatched his gaze away from her and took a

moment to refocus on the business he had to discuss. 'I'd like to talk to you about the outback tours. I know they've been your responsibility in the past.'

She looked surprised. 'I haven't been in charge of that area for a couple of years.'

'Quite. Dennis Ericson took over from you.'

'Yes.'

He pointed to the stack of hard-copy files on his desk and to the computer screen. 'I've been going through the company's history and I've noticed that the outback package tours used to be very popular but these days they aren't doing nearly as well as the tours to the reef and the rainforest. I'd like to hear your thoughts on that.'

'Oh...' Alice looked down at her hands and he could sense her discomfort.

He suspected it wouldn't be easy for her to give him an honest appraisal without implicating the staff member who'd taken control from her. Ericson.

'Well, to start with, the reef and the rainforest have more obvious and well-established attractions,' she said. 'That's where the big operators are and they're very strong in marketing and promoting their product. It's a lot easier to interest people in island cruises in glass-bottomed boats than in the hot and dusty outback.'

'But from what I've seen we used to connect tourists to a huge range of outback activities in the past. Everything from wilderness canoeing with helicopter drops to visiting Aboriginal communities and outback picnic races.'

Alice nodded. 'Actually, the farm stays and cattle musters were probably our most popular drawcards.'

'What happened to them?'

She gave a half-hearted shrug but didn't comment.

'I'd like you to be honest with me, Alice. It's important to get to the bottom of the problem. I expect growth in every area of my business.'

'But I'm not sure that I can help you.'

'Just tell me what you know.'

She sighed. 'There have been a few problems,' she admitted carefully. 'I'd say it started after we switched to a different airline for the charter flights out to the remote areas.'

Liam nodded. This change of airline, he was sure, had been Dennis's decision.

'The new company was much cheaper,' said Alice.

'But that economy came at a price?'

'Yes, they were too casual. Vague about timetables. Passengers were left stranded, luggage misplaced. And fair enough, we scored some bad word-of-mouth publicity.'

Liam nodded and made notes. 'What else?'

She tapped her pen against the cover of her notebook, taking her time before she replied. 'We used to have about fifty popular farm stays on our books and quite a few fishing spots up in the Gulf Country, but a lot of them pulled out.'

'Why?'

She hesitated. 'Haven't you already discussed this with Dennis?'

Liam had.

'I've taken note of Dennis's observations,' he said. 'But I'd like to hear your opinion.'

She frowned. 'Our outback contacts said it wasn't worth it.'

'Are you saying that they removed their properties from our books, or they dropped out of tourism altogether?'

It was clear she didn't want to answer this question. She opened her notebook, stared at a blank page, and then shut it again with a snap.

'Is that what happened?' Liam prompted again. 'These cattle stations stopped taking tourists?'

'No.'

Liam waited.

'They went to other tourist agencies.'

'Why?' he asked again.

Alice looked away and drew a sharp breath. 'I'm not sure.'

Now she was lying. He knew that, but he felt a grudging respect for her attempt to protect her colleague.

'Could it have been a PR problem?' he suggested carefully. 'Were a few toes stepped on? A few egos bruised?'

She looked directly at him and the loveliness of her soft grey eyes snagged at his breath.

Very carefully, she said, 'I guess it's easy sometimes for people in the city to misread country folk and to believe they haven't kept up with the times.'

'But that's rubbish. When it comes to market trends and meeting consumer demands, the people in the outback are as astute as anyone else.' He'd told Dennis Ericson as much.

He tapped long fingers on his desk top. 'As you might have guessed, I plan to turn this situation around. I'm going into the outback tomorrow to check things out. A kind of reconnaissance and goodwill tour.'

Alice nodded, her eyes watching him.

'I want you to come with me.'

The look of dismay that swept over her face shocked him, but he kept his face stone-hard.

His assessment of the company records showed a clear period of growth while Alice had been in charge of the outback operations. And after observing the way she handled his questions, he felt certain she had the diplomatic skills needed to win back lost clients— if that was still possible.

He cracked a small smile. 'Just remember I'm the boss and I get to make the decisions.'

His brashness fired two pink spots in her cheeks. 'I thought your first priority was to hunt down new premises. Somewhere flash on the Esplanade.'

'I've simply changed my priorities. As I see it now, my biggest problem is the outback and I'm going to tackle the most pressing problem first.'

Her hands twisted nervously. 'You know you shouldn't be asking me to do this, Liam. Take Shana. She's from Mount Isa and she has good contacts out west.'

'Shana's also a single parent with a rather emotionally fragile pre-school child.'

Her head shot up. 'You know about Toby?'

'Yes. You see, Alice, I have looked into alternatives.'

Her eyes widened and he thought he caught a flash of emotion. Annoyance? Pique? Was she miffed that he'd exhausted other possibilities before approaching her? The thought stirred him in ways that it shouldn't.

'Shana doesn't want to spend so much time away from her son,' he said. 'And Mary-Ann has specialised almost exclusively in the reef tours and attractions.'

'And Dennis?'

'I have other plans for him.' Liam pressed his point home. 'Alice, you used to look after the client base in the outback and it was doing well. It makes perfect sense that you should accompany me.'

There was a long, awkward silence and at the end of it she let out a sigh. Of defeat? Liam held his breath.

'I'm sorry, but I'd rather not,' she said quietly.

'I'm afraid you don't have any option. Alice, I'm telling you that this is not negotiable. It's a directive.'

'A directive?' Her eyes flashed with a mutinous glitter, but he glimpsed a flash of pain behind her defiance.

He felt a stab of guilt. Her husband had treated her shabbily and no doubt she found it hard to trust any man now, especially a man who'd deliberately sought her out, and then seduced her.

'How long would we be gone for?' she asked.

He forced a casual shrug. 'For as long as it takes.'

'Oh, for heaven's sake!' Her sudden anger launched her to her feet. 'What kind of answer is that?' Her eyes turned smoky, angry as thunderclouds. 'You might be my boss, Liam, but don't let the power go to your head. Surely you haven't forgotten *our* ground rules? You know perfectly well why we should make this trip as brief as possible.'

'Don't you trust me?' He tried to lighten the question with a chuckle, but even to his ears it sounded hollow—rather destroying the effect.

Her chin tilted to a haughty angle. 'No. Under the circumstances, I think I'd be foolish to trust you.'

Liam knew he deserved that. For a long moment, he stared at the surface of his desk while he breathed in and out slowly. Then he kept his gaze determined as he looked at her.

'Three days, Alice. That's all I'm asking.' God knew how he was going to survive three days in the outback without touching her, but he was determined to stand by his word.

'There'll be separate accommodation?'

'Of course. You have my word this will be strictly business.'

Her response was another venomous glare. 'You'd better believe it, Mr Conway.'

'What's this? A new dress code for the office?'

Alice squirmed beneath Dennis's scrutiny of her bone-coloured stretch Capri trousers and plain white scoop-neck T-shirt.

'I'm heading to the bush today,' she said, nodding to the small backpack on the floor beside her desk. 'Just for a quick tour of the Gulf Country to try to recoup some of the market share.'

'On your own?'

'With…the boss.'

'Oh? I see.' Dennis's voice added layers of innuendo to those simple words.

'So the boss's taking *you* out west? Just the two of you?' This came from Mary-Ann, who'd just come into the room.

Alice suppressed a sigh. 'Yes.'

These awkward questions could have been avoided if she'd been able to meet Liam at the airport, but he'd insisted on leaving from the office in full view of the staff. 'I don't want to skulk away as if we have something to hide,' he'd said.

'Shana won't be too happy,' said Mary-Ann.

Alice frowned at her. 'I thought Shana didn't want to go.'

'She didn't at first, because of Toby. But apparently the boss seemed really keen to take her and Shana went all jammy. I think she's developed a crush on him. Anyway, she ran around madly until she found a babysitter Toby really likes and she was all hot to trot.'

'When was this?' Alice tried to ignore nasty niggles of jealousy.

'Day before yesterday.'

Before yesterday… Goose-pimples broke out on Alice's arms. 'Did Shana tell Liam—I mean, Mr Conway—that she'd found someone to mind Toby?'

Mary-Ann nodded. 'First thing yesterday morning. But he said he'd already made alternative arrangements.'

Dennis made a show of rolling his eyes. 'Alternative arrangements aka Our Sweet Alice.'

Alice felt her face grow hot. Liam had spoken to her late yesterday morning, which meant he'd lied when he told her that Shana wasn't available.

How dared he lie? After the lofty way he'd talked about giving her his word, he'd been dishonest. She couldn't bear it.

Bending to hide her bright red face, she retrieved

her backpack and hooked it over one shoulder. 'Maybe not,' she muttered and marched out of the office and into the foyer.

Through the sliding glass doors she saw a limousine waiting outside on the semicircular drive. Liam, dressed in jeans and a casual light blue shirt, was standing on the footpath, chatting with the driver as if they were old friends.

A limo. Yikes.

The automatic doors opened for her, and the men looked in her direction.

'Ah, Ms Madigan,' said Liam, directing a courteous, almost remote smile her way.

'May I have a word with you, Mr Conway?'

'Yes, sure.' He frowned at her. 'What's the problem?'

She glanced at the driver and then at Liam. 'I don't think I can come on this trip.'

Liam's frown deepened. 'But you're all ready to go.'

How obtuse could the man be? 'Can we discuss this inside?'

With a stiff nod he followed her back through the sliding doors and into his office.

As soon as they were safely out of earshot she challenged him. 'You lied.'

'I beg your pardon?'

'Why did you tell me that Shana wasn't available?'

Liam closed his eyes and let out a low groan of exasperation. Then his eyes flashed open again. 'You're convinced I've rigged this so I can get you back into bed, aren't you?'

Alice gasped. *Get you back into bed…* The words

were like missiles. Damn him. How could he use their intimate encounter as a weapon? How could he turn it against her, as if she was the one in the wrong? Was he trying to distract her?

'I—I just want to know why you lied to me,' she cried.

'Listen, Alice, if you think that one night we spent together gives you the right to question every business decision I make you're going to come a cropper.'

She wanted to throw something at him. Was this the same man who'd made such exquisite love to her? Were all men toads? She almost cried at the thought. 'So,' she said, letting her bitterness show, 'first you lie to me and now you threaten me.'

His jaw clenched stubbornly. 'Don't forget you're on probation like any employee here. As far as this trip is concerned, I've decided that you're the most suitable person for the exercise and that's my sole reason for selecting you. How many times do you want me to tell you you're perfectly safe from me?'

She was so angered by his high-handed manner she couldn't respond.

'I won't come near you unless you ask me to, Ms Madigan.'

Her chin snapped high. 'Well, that won't happen in this lifetime.'

'Good,' he said. 'That's settled, then. Now let's get going. The charter pilot's ready and waiting at the airport.'

CHAPTER FOUR

WHEN the small charter plane took off it climbed to the east, taking Alice and Liam out over the shimmering, aquamarine waters of the Coral Sea before arching back towards the curving rim of the coastline. From their eagle-eye view, the sandy beaches below formed scalloped yellow trims on a string of pretty blue bays. Then the suburbs of Cairns spread out below them, reaching into an imposing hinterland of mountains clad in a thousand lush shades of green.

Liam, sitting on the far side of the narrow aisle, seemed to be entranced. He strained forward against his seat belt, eager to catch every detail of the spectacle below.

Alice had seen this view many times, but she never tired of it. She liked to imagine how it must look to international tourists used to the softer, more subtle landscapes of the northern hemisphere. Small wonder they found the vibrant colours and luxuriant vegetation of tropical Queensland exotic and exciting.

But as the small craft continued to climb she sank back into her seat and took a deep breath, closed her eyes for a minute or two. She had a faint headache which the confrontation in Liam's office hadn't helped. And last night she'd slept badly—thinking about this trip, and worrying about the strain of spending three whole days in her boss's exclusive company.

I won't come near you unless you ask me to.

Huh. In his dreams.

Problem was, if she was honest she had to admit that she hadn't slept well since the night of her birthday. *Their* birthday.

Darn it. She was still finding it impossible to put that night behind her. By the end of three days her nerves would be in shreds. How dared Liam trick her into this no-choice position?

Keeping her eyes closed, she tried to relax, deliberately loosening her shoulders, her stomach, her hands. She wasn't going to let Liam Conway upset her. After her divorce she'd vowed never to let another man undermine her confidence the way her husband had. She'd learned her lesson.

The important thing to remember was that her boss recognised how good she was at her job and, more importantly, he understood how significant the outback was to the company. It would be a real coup to bring the outback tours back on board.

Opening her eyes again, she sent a sleepy glance around the small cabin.

Liam was still intent on the scenery below. She watched the pilot, Joe Banyo, flick one of the many buttons on his complicated control panel, and saw him reach into a pack beside him for a roll of antacid tablets. From beneath heavy eyelids she watched him tear the foil and pop one into his mouth.

Joe turned, caught her watching him and sent her a quick, reassuring grin.

The monotonous, throaty roar of the plane's motor filled the cabin. She'd always found the surround-sound hum of small planes rather hypnotic and she let her eyes drift closed again. They were heading for Redhead Downs, about an hour and a half inland. Why not take a nap? It would kill two birds with one stone. She could get rid of her headache, and she could avoid the embarrassment of having Liam ignore her.

Turning sideways, she nestled more comfortably into the padded upholstery.

'Alice!'

Liam was shouting at her, shaking her shoulder roughly. 'Wake up!'

She blinked. And then her eyes flicked wide. Liam had already moved on past her and was at the front of the plane. He was crouching over Joe, the pilot, who was—oh, *good heavens*—slumped sideways in his harness.

Oh, my God, who was flying the plane? A blast of panic brought her fully awake.

'What's happened?' she shouted.

'He's collapsed.'

She stared in horror at Liam's shocked expression and the pilot's pale form. Oh, God. Flicking open her seat belt, she jumped to her feet. 'Have you tried to wake him?'

'Of course. He won't respond.'

'Is—is he breathing?'

'Hard to tell. I don't think so.'

They were going to crash! She struggled beneath another slam of panic. 'Is there a pulse?'

Liam flashed her a quick, worried frown and then touched his fingers to Joe's neck. 'I—I can't feel anything, but I'm not sure if I'm on the right spot.'

She tried to remember what she'd learned in various first-aid courses. 'Feel to the left of his Adam's apple.' *Please, Joe, have a heartbeat!* Her own heart was a sledgehammer.

Liam tried and shook his head. 'I'm not getting anything.' He struggled with Joe's harness. 'I'll have to get him out of this seat.'

Alice sent a hasty, terrified glance out of the nearest porthole to the grassy paddocks and bush below. Miles and miles below. At least the plane wasn't doing anything dreadful like spiralling downwards the way they did in war movies.

'Do you think he's had a heart attack?' She knew she sounded panicky.

'How the hell would I know?'

She remembered seeing the antacid Joe had taken earlier. Had he taken it because he'd felt chest pain and thought he had indigestion? If he'd had a heart attack, they would have to get help fast or he would die. Oh, God, what was she thinking? They were all going to die if their pilot couldn't land the plane.

In the confined space it was a terrible struggle but at last Liam managed to drag Joe and together they set him in the tiny aisle, on his side in the recovery position.

'You'll have to look after him, while I try to get help on the radio,' Liam told her.

'OK,' she said, thinking she would need to be a contortionist to attempt CPR in the available space. 'I'll do my best.'

'Good girl.'

She looked up quickly. Liam's face was pale, his

expression grim—just this side of terrified—but he managed a reassuring smile.

'I don't suppose you know how to fly a plane?' she asked.

''Fraid not. But the plane must be set on autopilot. We don't seem to have lost altitude, so that gives us a bit of leeway while we try for some help.'

She gave a brief nod, an even briefer smile. 'Good luck.'

He was already climbing into the pilot's seat, and she turned her attention to the unconscious man. He needed mouth-to-mouth resuscitation and CPR. She hoped to God she could remember the procedure.

She checked Joe's airway and began to breathe for him. After the initial weirdness of putting her mouth to a stranger's, she settled into the rhythm. One breath every four seconds.

'Mayday! Mayday!' Liam was shouting.

How scary those words sounded. But at least he'd figured out how to work the radio.

Alice wished she was braver. She knew she mustn't think about the plane crashing, but horrific images of their tiny cabin smashing into hard earth kept jumping into her head.

Don't let your mind go there! Get a grip! Be disciplined. Focus on Joe, on the breathing.

She could hear Liam shouting to someone, explaining about their pilot's collapse. Thank heavens he'd made contact. She felt a tiny bit calmer. And remembered to pray.

'We're close to Redhead Downs,' Liam was saying, and then he gave their position from a control-panel monitor and reeled off a string of numbers—something to do with the plane.

She finished a round of breathing and checked again for the pilot's pulse. Beneath her fingertips, she felt a tiny beat. Dear God, thank you. She wouldn't need to apply CPR. But Joe still wasn't breathing, so she began again on another round of mouth-to-mouth.

'OK,' Liam was shouting into the radio. 'I've found the airspeed dial. It says we're flying at—er—one hundred and twenty knots. Is that OK? It is? Great!'

Alice kept up the rhythmic breathing. Surely Joe would revive soon? As she worked she could hear the voice on the radio explaining the basic controls to Liam, and the confident replies Liam gave to each set of instructions. Wow! How did he stay so calm?

In the midst of terror, there was something commanding about his manner, something reassuring. Perhaps it was an illusion created by broad shoulders?

But the illusion was destroyed when Liam yelled, 'Brace yourself back there. We're already approaching the Redhead Downs airstrip. I'm going to have to land this thing soon.'

Alice's chest squeezed like a vice, breaking the rhythm of her breathing. She had a vision of the ground racing up to meet them, fancied she heard the shriek of ripping metal, the blast of an explosion. Pain.

Idiot, stop that right now!

She heard a faint groan and stared hard at Joe. Had he made that noise? Was his colour improving? Surely he looked a little pinker?

He groaned again and coughed.

'Joe's alive!' she screamed.

Liam was too busy focusing on instructions from the radio to reply.

Joe clutched at his stomach.

'He's coming round,' shouted Alice.

'Can he talk?' Liam called back to her.

Alice gave the poor man a shake. 'Hey, Joe, wake up. We need you!'

'Ask him if the plane has fixed or retractable landing gear,' yelled Liam.

'Joe,' Alice shouted. 'What kind of landing gear does this plane have?'

There was no reply. Joe's face was pale again and beaded with sweat.

'Please, Joe,' urged Alice. 'Tell me about the landing gear.'

'Fixed,' he whispered.

'Fixed,' she called back to Liam.

'Fixed,' Liam shouted into the radio. 'Hallelujah! We've got wheels!'

His excitement was contagious. Suddenly it seemed possible that somehow Liam was going to land this plane. They were going to be all right. Alice felt a surge of courage. She was going to have faith. Now. Even when poor Joe rolled onto his side and groaned wretchedly, she remained calm.

She found a hand towel and a bottle of water in her backpack and washed his face. His eyes flickered open.

'Sorry about this. Think it must be food poisoning.' And then he tried to sit up. 'I'm all right now. I'll take over.' But he'd no sooner spoken than his face turned as white as paper and he sank backwards again, clutching his stomach.

'If you try to fly and keep blacking out we won't make it, Joe. The best way you can help is by lying still and staying conscious. That way, Liam can ask you questions.'

Eyes closed, he nodded.

She dampened the towel again and mopped the beads of perspiration on his brow, and as she worked she watched Liam in her periphery.

From her point of view he looked perfectly cool and collected, but she knew that was impossible. He'd never flown a plane before. He would be fighting fear every second.

'I can see the landing strip now,' he was telling his instructor on the radio and he sounded remarkably calm. 'Yes, I'm pulling back on the throttle, reducing power. Yes.'

Joe grabbed Alice's elbow. 'Tell him he mustn't let the nose drop more than six inches below the horizon.'

She relayed the message at the top of her voice.

'Doing my best,' was Liam's grim-voiced reply.

She could feel the plane's descent and panic rose again, but she pushed it away from her. She had faith in Liam Conway. He was going to make this. They were going to be safe.

Joe's eyes were shut and she wondered if he'd fainted again, but when the sound of the motor suddenly changed his eyes opened and his head snapped back.

'Pull all the way back on the throttle,' he shouted.

'Pull all the way back on the throttle,' Alice repeated.

'I'm pulling!'

This time Liam sounded really worried. Alice could see the tension in his shoulders, the strain in the back of his neck.

Through the windscreen in front of him, she saw the airstrip, tilted at an alarmingly rakish angle, zooming closer, closer.

She almost jumped out of her skin when Joe's hand grabbed her wrist. 'You should have your seat belt on,' he said.

'What about you?'

'I can't bloody move. I'll be OK down here.' He was grasping the legs of seats on either side of the aisle. 'You get in a seat. Quick!'

The plane teetered back to the correct level as Alice scrambled into her seat and buckled up. Oh, God, they were almost touching the ground. She wanted to yell to Liam that he could do this, but her throat was too jam-packed with fear. Besides, she knew he was listening intently to the person talking him down on the radio.

She held her breath.

The hard red dirt of the outback airstrip was so close now. Coming closer every second.

She shut her eyes as the wheels skimmed the earth. They bumped and bounced off again and then reconnected with a rough thump that almost jolted her out of her seat. Oxygen masks tumbled out of overhead lockers as their tiny craft bounced and streaked at breakneck speed along the rough airstrip. Alice didn't dare to breathe.

On the floor beside her lay Joe, his face contorted with pain and the effort of holding himself in place.

But they were slowing. Yes, they were definitely slowing. They were alive and the plane…was… coming… to a stop.

'You did it!' she screamed, rushing over to Liam.

He turned as she reached him and he looked pale and shell-shocked, as if he didn't quite believe he'd made it.

'That was just fantastic!' she cried, throwing her arms about him and hugging his shoulders.

'Thanks,' he said. 'But I think we'd better get out of here fast. God knows what I've done to the plane.'

She stepped back quickly, realising that her celebration was premature.

'You get out while I get the pilot,' he said.

'I'll help you.'

'No, you look after the door.'

Right. Alice turned to the door and saw the complicated handle. Oh, heck. How on earth was she supposed to open it? For a moment she felt embarrassingly useless—especially when Liam had been so amazingly resourceful—but then she noticed a helpful sign and a diagram.

Liam hauled Joe's arm over one shoulder and got him to his feet, but the poor fellow only took a few steps then folded, so in the end Liam had to carry him out and they settled him on the ground in the shade of a bush.

Shading her eyes against the glare, Alice saw two four-wheel-drive vehicles scorching towards them, their cabins barely showing above clouds of billowing red dust.

Minutes later they were being congratulated and slapped on the back by Bob and Noreen King, the owners of Redhead Downs, and their head stockman, Blade Finch.

'Bloody well done, mate,' Bob said to Liam. 'Civil Aviation called to warn us and said you'd never flown a plane before.'

'We made it, that's the main thing.' Liam nodded towards Joe and Alice, who was kneeling beside him. 'I'm worried about the pilot.'

'I think he's fainted again,' said Alice. 'He needs urgent attention.'

'Flying doc's on his way, love,' said Noreen. 'We're in luck. He was holding a clinic not far away, but actually…' She walked over to Joe and he opened his eyes and gave a weak smile '…it looks like you've done the doctor's job for him.'

Now that it was over, Alice realised that her headache was pounding, but she managed a smile. And then she looked at Liam and felt a savage little twist in her chest when she saw that his hands were trembling.

But he quickly stuffed them into his jeans pockets and flashed her a reassuring smile.

CHAPTER FIVE

HE'D almost killed them. If the nose of the plane had tipped a fraction lower...

He'd almost killed Alice. He'd forced her, against her will, to come on this trip to the outback and then he'd almost killed her.

A blind, suffocating horror hit Liam almost as soon as his feet touched the ground. He felt his knees give way, but somehow he managed to shove the horror aside and stay upright.

It was later that the enormity of their near-death experience really took him by the throat, after the flying doctor left with the sick pilot, *en route* for Mount Isa Hospital.

Bob and Noreen King plied them with hot, sweet tea and thick corned-beef and tomato sandwiches and showed them to their guest accommodation—cute log cabins, separate as requested, down by a billabong.

It was there, once Liam was alone in his cabin— and he thanked God that he was alone—that he broke down, shaking violently, almost weeping with the shock of knowing how close they'd come. So close to death.

Again.

He knew from guilty experience how very fragile life was, had learned first-hand the heartless ease with which a life could be lost in one moment of reck-lessness.

All the images he'd tried to suppress came flooding back—the lifeless body and twisted metal. One careless split-second. That was all it took to measure the distance between existence and death. He'd learned that dreadful lesson years ago, when he was twenty-one, but still the guilt lived on.

So close. Today they'd come so terribly close.

The black horror of it crowded in, dragging him down, as it had so many times before.

Hauling off his clothes, he stumbled into the shower and let the warm water pour over him, let the familiar pinprick of fine needles heat his skin. He wasn't sure how long he was there, sagging against the tiled wall of the recess, but at some point the voice of reason finally began to make itself heard.

The thought gradually sank in that on this occasion no lives had been lost. Today he'd actually saved lives.

He clung to that knowledge. But it still wasn't enough to reassure him.

A knock sounded on the door of his cabin.

'Be with you in a moment,' he called as he shut off the water and reached for a towel. Hastily he thrust his legs into jeans and roughly towelled his damp hair as he crossed the room.

Alice stood on his doorstep, showered and changed into khaki shorts and a cute white top. Her eyes were huge in her pale face, and he realised with a slam of guilt that he'd been too self-absorbed to check how she was coping with the after-shock of their ordeal.

'I'm sorry,' she said, eyeing his state of undress, his ruffled, damp hair. 'I've interrupted you.'

'Nothing important's happening here.' He flipped the towel over one shoulder.

Just the same, she looked uncomfortable. She lowered her gaze, as if his bare chest bothered her, and he tried to ignore the way the tiny shoestring straps on her top revealed the exquisite perfection of her collar-bones, the way the stretch material hugged her breasts.

She waved a vague hand at the billabong. Their cabins were set on its banks, giving them a pretty view of silky, tea-coloured water almost completely covered by pink water lilies. It was encircled by towering, shady paperbark trees and lush pandanus palms.

'So what do you think of the guest accommodation on Redhead Downs?' she asked him.

'Fabulous setting.' He watched a solitary white heron fish the opposite bank, its long beak probing beneath the lily pads. Then he stepped back, pushing his door wider open. 'And the cabins are adequate. Why don't you come in?'

She looked uncertain. 'I just wanted to make sure you're OK.'

'I'm fine. Come on, come on in.'

It was only when she hesitated again that he remembered. 'Whoa! Almost forgot. All the drama must have fused my brain. We're keeping our distance, aren't we?'

Whose idea had that been? His?

She looked up at him again and this time her gorgeous grey eyes were shiny with tears. 'I haven't thanked you properly,' she said. 'You were so amazing. I—I don't know how you landed that plane. It was a very brave thing to do.'

'That wasn't bravery. I was working on pure adrenaline. Anyway, what about your first aid? You saved the pilot's life. The flying doctor said as much.'

She shrugged. 'My contribution wouldn't have been much use if the plane had crashed.' A tear trembled on the end of an eyelash, slipped down her cheek.

Liam reached over and caught it with the tip of his forefinger.

'Sorry,' she said, blinking hard and releasing more tears.

'Don't be. It's natural to be upset after a shock like that.' What a hypocrite he was, pretending to be the cool, nerveless hero.

Alice wiped her cheeks with her fingers and gave a little shiver, and then she hugged herself, rubbing her hands over her bare arms.

Watching her hands, he couldn't resist asking, 'You want me to do that?'

She stared at him, her mouth parted, her eyes damp, her lashes spiky and wet. 'What?' But then she looked down at her arms wrapped across her front. 'Yes,' she whispered so softly he only just caught it. 'I—I need a hug.'

His breathing snagged.

Once more her eyes lifted, met his and signalled a silent message. Blood throbbed in his veins, pounded in his ears. There it was; the insane chemistry they'd felt on the night they met. The urge he'd been fighting ever since. Now it triggered a violent wanting in him, an echoing tremble in her.

'Alice, come here.'

She needed no further invitation. She floated through the doorway and into his arms. With his foot he closed the cabin door behind them.

Her body seemed to merge into his, her arms linked around him and her mouth, her sweet, sweet mouth opened to him in a kiss that was one hundred per cent distilled passion.

Liam was already lost. Lost in the need to touch and to taste and to hold her.

'I'm so glad we're alive,' she whispered as she pressed eager kisses over his face.

He knew their emotions were sweeping common sense aside. Alice was overwhelmed by relief and gratitude, he by his desire and his need to blank out dark memories. But as he framed her face with his hands, as her lips parted beneath his, inviting him into her, he knew that he was a mere man, and he'd wanted this woman, had craved her ever since the night they'd met and made love.

Today they'd come face to face with the cruel mystery of chance. They'd been courted by death and had escaped its claws. And now they needed to embrace life. They needed this assurance, this coming together of warm bodies, of wildly beating hearts.

The touch of Alice's hands on his body made his heart jolt so fiercely it practically wedged in his throat. And her hands were merciless as they explored his shoulders, as her fingers made circles on his chest.

Then the flats of her palms slid down his sides to his hips, to the waistband of his jeans, and he gave up all attempts to justify this pleasure. This was OK. Very OK.

But just as he slipped his hands beneath her top, he remembered.

God help him, he remembered the one thing that couldn't be overlooked.

'Wait, Alice. Alice, wait.' With an anguished groan he closed his hands around hers just as she reached the snap fastener on his jeans.

'Wait?' She sounded breathless and embarrassed and she buried her face into his chest.

'I didn't bring anything with me.'

Her head shot up. 'I don't understand. What are you talking about?'

'Protection.' He let out a deep, ragged sigh. 'We weren't going to do this. I gave you my word and I deliberately didn't pack anything, so there'd be no chance of weakening.'

'Oh.' She wriggled her hands out of his grasp and pressed them to her bright pink cheeks.

'I'm sorry,' he said.

'Actually, it doesn't matter.'

'Don't be silly. Of course it does.'

Alice smiled at him. 'Don't look so worried, Liam. I'm safe as houses. We don't need protection.'

What was she implying? That she was on the Pill?

'I'm not going to get pregnant,' she said and she forced a careless little laugh.

The brittle, offhand way she said this made her look and sound tough, but Liam could sense vulnerability lying just below the surface. He stepped towards her and reached for her hand.

Watching the way their fingers linked, she said softly, 'I know pregnancy isn't the only reason couples use protection.'

'I've—I've never taken risks. I would never put you at risk, Alice.'

'Well, you're the only man I've slept with apart from my husband.'

Was she telling him as clearly as she could that she wanted to take up where they'd left off? The thought robbed him of breath. 'So you think—'

'Yes,' she said, looking up at him with a sweet, shy smile. 'I think. I very definitely think.'

This time when they kissed it was different. Not just because the kiss was slow and long and lush and warm, but because now they were no longer swept away by dangerously high emotions. They'd taken a step back; they'd had a chance for second thoughts, to think of the consequences. They'd given each other the space to say no.

And they'd both chosen yes.

This time as Liam's fingertips roamed the silky smooth skin at Alice's waist his desire was buoyed by a surge of relief. To hell with office politics. He was mad about this woman. He wanted her, and he didn't care who knew it.

It was late afternoon. The sun was a red ball, hanging hot and low in the west, reaching beneath the branches of the paperbark outside Liam's cabin and spreading a warm pool of light over the bed where they'd fallen asleep.

Alice woke first. For a while she lay still, thinking about how precious life was, how amazing and unpredictable. And the man whose limbs were entwined with hers was precious, amazing and unpredictable, too.

She suspected that she was in love.

She knew that most people would tell her it was impossible to really love someone on such a short acquaintance. Surely after her experience with Todd she should be more cautious? But she'd never felt like this about Todd. Even before he'd started cheating on her, he'd never really fired her admiration, or her passion.

Liam had. And if what she felt for him wasn't love it was so close to the real thing she couldn't tell the difference.

Carefully she lifted his arm and slipped out of bed, pulled on her top and pants and switched on the electric kettle. The sound of the water bubbling to the boil woke Liam and he rolled onto his side and squinted against the shaft of sunlight as he watched her.

'There are tea bags or instant coffee,' she said. 'Which would you like?'

'I'll go for coffee, thanks.'

Yawning, he stood, stretched and rummaged in his pack for boxer shorts, while Alice brought their mugs back to the bed and set them on a side-table, then piled the pillows into a comfortable mound and settled herself just so.

Liam sat on the edge of the bed with one leg bent, resting on the mattress.

She handed him his mug, and for a minute or two they sipped their drinks in silence.

'Why the worried frown?' Liam asked her suddenly.

'Was I frowning?' Alice deliberately relaxed her face. 'I was thinking about us,' she admitted.

'And that makes you frown?'

'Not really. I was just wondering—'

'If we should have sex again now or after our coffee?' Liam supplied with a grin.

Smiling, Alice shook her head. 'Actually, I was wondering if we're better at physical intimacy than we are at every-day conversation.'

Liam grinned again. 'We haven't had much chance for every-day conversation.'

'No, we've gone about this backwards.'

'You think so?'

'Well, normally when a man meets a woman...' She hesitated. 'Mind you, I'm out of touch when it comes to dating. Maybe it was only in the Dark Ages that people went out for some time and got to know each other before they—'

'Leapt into bed?'

'Yes.'

Liam set his mug back on the little table beside the bed. Her foot was near his knee and he casually wrapped his hand around it. 'We can always back up a step or two and try the getting-to-know-you part. Although I already know a lot of important things about you.'

'You think so?'

'Absolutely.'

'What kinds of things?'

His long brown fingers played with her big toe. 'You like green.'

Alice rolled her eyes. 'And how relevant is that to a relationship?'

'It's vital. I might hate green.'

'But you don't, do you?' She regretted the hopeful note that crept into her voice.

'Green's fine with me, but that's only because I have a very liberal attitude to colour.'

'Does this liberal attitude allow you to have a favourite colour?'

He thought about this and smiled. 'I'm quite partial to white.'

'White?' She grinned. 'Is that because you're a Virgo?'

'I don't know. Perhaps…'

She was about to tease him, but changed her mind when she realised that his smile had turned cheeky and he was paying rather obvious attention to her white top and white silk and lace pants.

'Now,' said Liam, playing with her next toe, creating ripples of warmth that swam up her leg. 'I know you're only recently divorced.'

'Yes…well…that's not my favourite topic. If you like we can skip over that one.'

Liam watched her thoughtfully for a moment.

She didn't want to think about Todd now, when she'd been feeling so peaceful and happy.

'You started this, remember?'

'You're worlds apart from him, Liam. In every way. In all the best ways.'

He accepted this without comment, although she was sure she saw his neck redden. He moved on to her next toe, circling the ball of it with his finger tip. 'You spend far too much time reading in bed.'

'You know that because you saw the pile of books in my bedroom. Not fair. You have an advantage; you've been to my house.'

She wriggled her foot in his hand and he tightened his grasp. 'I didn't realise this was a competition.'

'It's not a competition. It's just that…' She sat up, chewing her bottom lip as she struggled to find the right words for the niggle of disquiet inside her.

'I still feel as if there's too much I don't know about you.'

'Ask away. What do you want to know? You want me to start with my blood group?'

Letting out a noisy sigh, she slumped back on the pile of pillows. 'Don't make a joke of this, please.'

He let her foot go. 'OK. I can see there's something bothering you, so why don't you get it off your chest?'

The cabin and the surrounding bush seemed incredibly quiet as he waited for her.

'Can I trust you?' she asked.

She could see immediately that her question upset him.

'I would hope so, Alice. What makes you doubt it?'

'Well…'

There seemed to be a shadow in Liam's past that bothered her, but the feeling was so tenuous she couldn't be sure and it would be nosy to push him when they'd only just met, so she took a more obvious route. 'There's the business about Shana.'

His mouth pulled into a guilty grimace and then he reached for her foot again and with his thumb he rubbed her instep. 'OK, confession time.' He stroked her skin ever so slowly.

Did he have any idea what that did to her?

'You're dead right. I wasn't completely honest. But

you see, when I first asked Shana to come on this trip and she said she couldn't I was really pleased. It meant I had a genuine excuse to ask you.' He lifted her foot and dropped a warm kiss in the curve of her arch. 'You were the right person for the job.'

There was a sound of knocking on the cabin next door, the cabin assigned to Alice. She stiffened and tried to pull her foot from his grasp. Was someone looking for her?

Liam ignored the knock. 'All along it was you I really wanted,' he said.

'I—I see.' She supposed she should still be angry with him. Problem was, she knew now that she liked being wanted by Liam Conway. She liked it very much, thank you.

There was another knock, on Liam's door this time.

'Coming,' he called, and he dropped one last kiss on her foot before crossing the room to answer it.

He didn't open the door very wide, but Alice caught a quick glimpse of Noreen King holding a cane hamper.

'I've brought your meals,' she said.

'Oh. Wonderful. Thanks very much.'

'I knocked on Alice's door, but there didn't seem to be anyone around, so is it all right if I leave her meal here with you?' There was no mistaking the curiosity in her voice.

'Yes,' said Liam. 'Yes, that's fine. I'll pass it on to her.' Then he remembered to ask, 'Do you have any news from the flying doctor?'

'Oh, yes. They said Joe's making a good recovery. And he's been singing your praises to anyone who'll listen.'

'He should be singing Alice's praises. She's the one who attended to him.'

After Liam had thanked her again for the food, he closed the door and came back into the room. 'I'd say we've been sprung.' His tell-tale smile suggested that he didn't mind at all. 'Now, let's see what we have to eat. I'm starving.'

Alice wanted to keep their conversation going. Liam had only just started to open up. She wanted to know so much more about him. And at some point she knew she should probably tell him about her problems with infertility.

But Liam was already opening the hamper and she realised that she was hungry.

'Smells fantastic,' she said.

They fell on the hamper with the eagerness of children scrambling for cookies after a long day at school. They found a bottle of red wine, a selection of cheeses, freshly baked bread rolls, a crisp green salad and a wonderfully aromatic country-style casserole.

'Now, this is service,' beamed Liam. 'We've got to get this property back on our books.'

Alice pulled on shorts and hurried about the cabin's tiny kitchenette, finding plates and wine glasses and cutlery. 'There's a little table and chairs outside. We could eat out there and watch the sunset,' she suggested.

'Sounds terrific.'

It was. The setting was perfect. The sky to the west was a riot of red and orange, gilding the surface of the billabong while purple shadows crept across it from the trees at its edge. The food was delicious and the wine mellow. And, to Alice's surprise and delight,

Liam opened up. She wondered why she'd ever worried that they might not find things to talk about.

They talked easily. They talked about Liam's vision for the company, about the places they'd travelled to and their favourite animals, music, food. They delved more deeply into things they had in common, too, like a fondness for the outback. They discovered that they shared an impatience with having to line up in queues, and, of course, there was their shared birthday.

When Alice raised that topic she fancied she saw a flash of pain in Liam's eyes and she tried to remember if it was the same emotion she'd glimpsed briefly at the Hippo Bar when they'd first discovered that their birthdays were on the same day.

But like that other time the fleeting sadness came and went so quickly she might have been imagining things, especially when Liam seemed as keen to talk about their birthday as she was.

'It blows me away,' she said. 'Just think. When we were kids, whenever I woke up, all excited on my birthday morning, you were waking up, too. You were looking forward to your presents the same as I was.' She shook her head, smiling. 'Back then I was always so proud of being another year older, but I'm afraid that's going to change from now on.'

'Now you've turned oops,' he said, remembering.

'Yes.' They shared a smile. 'So, tell me...' she said. 'Which was your happiest birthday?'

His eyes held hers. 'This year's would take some beating.'

'Apart from that.'

Hooking an elbow over the back of his chair, he

looked out at the thin slice of red-gold sun that glowed like the embers of a fire above the dark hills on the horizon. 'I'd have to say my eighteenth was the best. I was on holiday at Kirra on the Gold Coast.'

'Your eighteenth,' said Alice. 'I would have been twelve.' Her eyes widened. 'Hey! That's amazing. I was at Kirra then, too. My family went down to the Gold Coast for the September holidays and we rented a beach house at Kirra.'

They stared at each other for a long moment, smiling as they thought about the possibilities.

'We might have both been on the beach at the same time,' she said. 'We might have seen each other.'

She was totally caught up with the romance of it. She could picture Liam on the beach—a tall, dark, bronzed and handsome surfer boy. If he'd seen her then, would he have fallen for her?

Get real. She was twelve. She sighed. 'You wouldn't have noticed me, of course.'

'I'm sure I would have. I bet you were an exceptionally cute twelve-year-old.'

She shook her head. 'You would have been too busy chasing after the older girls in their bikinis.'

'I'm noticing you now.' His blue eyes gently teased her.

Oh, man. Her intense response to the way Liam looked at her knocked the questions she still wanted to ask clear out of her head. Minutes earlier she'd been wondering how the son of a struggling orchard farmer had become the owner of a huge multimillion-dollar business, and why, at the age of thirty-six, such a charming, attractive man was still unmarried. And suddenly none of that mattered.

What mattered was the way Liam was looking at her. Todd had never, ever looked at her with that hungry heat, had never made her feel like the most desirable woman in the world.

And Liam's touch really mattered. Just thinking about the magic of his hands on her body made her skin flame and tingle all over. Liam turned her into a love goddess with his very first caress. Right now, all that mattered was that tonight, all night, she would be sharing his bed.

The sound of Bob King calling to his dogs woke Liam next morning. This was followed by unnecessarily loud banging sounds and then stomping footsteps approaching the cabins.

'I think our host wants to let us know we have company,' Liam told Alice as he swung out of bed.

He was dressed and at the door by the time Bob knocked.

Bob grinned at him. 'I came down to warn you that a pack of journalists are on their way to interview the big hero.'

Liam groaned. 'They're not trying to make out *I'm* a hero, are they?'

'Of course they are, mate. A charter plane and a helicopter left Cairns five minutes ago, so there must be a mob of them coming. Looks like you're going to be splashed all over the papers and the telly.' Bob rubbed his hands as if he couldn't believe his luck that he was hosting a celebrity.

Liam let out his breath on a noisy sigh. He'd been planning for him and Alice to continue their tour of the outback today but it sounded as if they were going to be delayed. 'All I did was follow a few instructions over the radio.'

'You can tell them that, but I reckon they'll still want to make something special out of you.' Bob chuckled. 'Crikey, mate, it's the truth. You are a hero. It's not every day that someone lands a plane without even a few basic lessons.'

When Liam came back into the cabin he wagged a finger at Alice. 'This is your fault,' he said. 'Whenever I'm with you I become a media magnet. First the *Cairns Post*, now national coverage.'

'Oh, no, you've caught me out.' Alice pouted in mock-dismay. 'I'll come quietly, officer. Yes, I poisoned poor Joe the pilot's food simply so Liam Conway could pull a hero stunt and wind up on the seven o'clock news.'

Liam grinned and then ploughed a hand through his hair as he considered his options. 'I suppose I could always turn this to the company's advantage.'

'Why not?' Alice nodded as she considered this. 'You may as well get some free publicity.'

'During the interviews I could mention the company name whenever possible and I can talk about our plans to revive Kanga Tours' services in this region.'

'Why don't you get them to do the interviews down here by the billabong? That setting would make a great backdrop.'

'Good idea.' He crossed the room to look again at the view and the wide expanse of bright morning sky. The lake wore the pink water lilies like a decorative shawl and the encircling trees with their tapering blue-green leaves and characteristic peeling papery bark were stunning.

It was a classic Australian bush setting. The kind of scene that tugged at the heartstrings of city-bound Australians, reminding them of their nostalgia for the outback, luring them away from their theatres and coffee shops to reconnect with this unique, almost primal landscape. The perfect tourism poster back-drop.

'You'll have to be prepared for the journalists to beat up the dangers of flying in small aeroplanes,' Alice reminded him.

Liam turned back from the window. She was sitting in the middle of the bed and she looked adorably, sensationally sexy with her dark curls tumbling about her shoulders while wearing nothing but a sheet. For a crazy moment, he wondered if there was time for him to climb back in there with her before the journalists arrived.

Get your brain into gear. Concentrate on the business at hand.

'I'll try to steer the talk away from the emergency and on to *why* we were flying in this amazing part of the country,' he said.

'But you won't be able to get out of being a hero, Liam.'

The special, dancing light in her eyes pulled at a cord deep within him. For one fantastic moment he could almost believe that he was a hero, *her* hero. But then, just as quickly, he remembered the grim truth. Liam Conway was anything but heroic.

How would Alice look at him when she discovered that?

CHAPTER SIX

'YOU know, there's bound to be a wife somewhere.'

Alice tried to ignore Shana's remark and kept typing.

Ever since yesterday afternoon, when she and Liam returned from their three days in the outback—their three incredible, mega-successful days—Shana had been doing her best to taunt Alice.

Now Shana left her desk and came to stand right next to Alice. 'A man with Liam Conway's looks and money can't reach his mid-thirties without a string of women chasing after him. And there has to have been at least one who got her hooks into him.'

Alice looked up and met her with a level gaze. 'I don't see that it's really our business.'

'Oh, come on.' Shana touched the petals of the single rose in the green vase on Alice's desk. 'You can't expect me to believe that it isn't *your* business.'

'I don't see—'

'You and Liam are an item, right?'

'Shana, really, I'd prefer not to—'

'Don't get all hot and bothered, Alice. Everyone in the office knows the answer. You tried to pull the wool over our eyes after the photo in the *Cairns Post*. We gave you the benefit of the doubt then. But we saw the way the boss was looking at you when you got back yesterday. The poor guy was practically drooling. The game's up, girlfriend.'

Alice sighed. It was pointless to deny it. And Liam had said he didn't care who knew that she was his woman. 'Well, yes. I suppose you could say we're an item.' But she knew that Shana had developed a crush on Liam and that sour grapes could be an issue. 'Just because we're an item doesn't mean I need to—'

'Marry him?' Shana finished for her.

'For heaven's sake!' Shaking her head, Alice reached for a folder in the filing cabinet beside her desk. 'I've only just met the man. I'm certainly not thinking very far into the future.'

'Oh, come on, Alice. Are you telling me that one of the wealthiest and best-looking men in the region is red hot for you and you haven't thought once about the long term?'

'That's exactly what I'm telling you.'

'Alice, I've discussed this with your workmates, who know you and love you. And we all agree you're a one-man girl. You haven't got it in you to flit from guy to guy. You fall heavily for a man and that's it.'

Alice sighed. 'Can I ask where this conversation is heading? Are you trying to warn me off Liam?'

Shana's eyes glinted knowingly, as if she was privy to a nasty secret, and Alice's stomach sank as she remembered her workmate's original question about whether there was a wife in Liam's past.

'If you've got something to tell me, spill it,' she said. 'Don't treat me like I'm a naïve teenager with stars in my eyes.' She'd just been through a horrible divorce, for heaven's sake. She wasn't going to rush into another mistake.

'Well, do you know whether or not the boss has been married?' Shana persisted.

'I know he's not married now, and that's good enough for me.' Alice was pleased that her voice was calm in spite of the frantic way her heart galloped.

She wasn't thrilled that Liam had not volunteered any information about the women in his past, but she'd decided not to press him. Instead she'd chosen to trust him. She'd trusted him from the first moment she met him in the Hippo Bar and so far he hadn't let her down.

Ah, yes, a smug inner voice whispered, *but you trusted Todd for years and years and look where that got you.*

'OK, can you answer this?' Shana asked. 'Why has Liam Conway never driven a motor car?'

'What?' Alice gaped at her. 'Are you crazy? Of course he drives cars. The man landed a plane, for heaven's sake.' And he'd produced his driver's licence as proof of his birthday on the night they met.

It was possible that Shana's smile was meant to be sympathetic, but it didn't quite work. 'The *Sydney Morning Herald* ran a story while you were away that questioned how Liam Conway could possibly land a plane when no one's ever seen him behind a steering wheel,' she said smugly.

'That's nonsense.' Shana was only trying to stir up trouble. 'Now, if you're quite finished, I have work to do.' She couldn't stomach any more of this conversation.

'I was only telling you this for your own good, but if you're bent on defending the man no matter what, I'm wasting my time.'

Letting out an angry sniff, Shana turned and flounced back to her desk and positioned her chair and computer screen so there was no chance of eye contact.

Good, Alice decided, noting the other woman's stiff, angry back. Now she could get on with her own work.

Movement at the bottom of her computer screen caught her eye and she saw a string of new email messages arrive.

Enquiries about the outback tours had been flooding in, thanks to the publicity Liam had attracted. He'd handled the media interviews brilliantly—was charming, articulate and perfectly comfortable in front of the cameras. And as a result they'd already drawn more interest in Kanga Tours than they'd dared to hope for.

It would be best to deal with the email messages quickly before she moved on to the list of phone calls she had to make. She scanned the email list and her heart bounced. One message leapt out from the screen—a private communication from Conway, Liam C.

Oh, heavens. Her skin flashed with nervous excitement as she clicked on it.

Can I invite myself to dinner at your place this evening? I'll bring takeaway and wine. What would you prefer—Indian, Thai, fish and chips, pizza? You name it, I'll find it.
Just have the green plates ready.
Missing you like crazy.
L

Alice felt her face burst into flames.

Missing you like crazy.

No way could she wipe the smile from her face. Thank heavens Shana wasn't looking her way.

Missing you like crazy.

Liam's mind was not on his work. He should have been dealing with everything that had piled up while he was away, but his concentration was shot to pieces. He couldn't stop thinking about Alice. He sat in his office, staring at his computer screen, hoping she wasn't too busy to answer his email immediately.

Missing you like crazy.

Perhaps he *was* crazy. Surely he was crazy to allow this to happen, to become so involved with a woman that he let her sidetrack him from his focus on his brand-new business enterprise.

He'd come to this city with a single-minded purpose, prepared to do everything that was needed to secure his company's viability. But from the very moment he'd seen Alice in the Hippo Bar, he'd been a marked man.

He hadn't believed it was possible to be so distracted, so obsessed. Alice was a miracle, his perfect woman. And to think he'd had to come way up north to find her. Right now all he could think about was this evening.

Please say yes, Alice.

Actually, in a perfect world he wouldn't wait till this evening. He would summon Alice to his office, lock the door and explore the possibilities his wide desk offered. But of course that wasn't going to happen, so he kept picturing other fantasies about tonight—the way he would rush through Alice's front door, dump the takeaway food on her kitchen counter and start to undress her.

Say yes, Alice. The only possible answer is a big, fat yes.

Alice stared at the message from her boss, thinking thoughts so lusty and steamy she could hardly sit still.

All it took was a few words on a screen—*Missing you like crazy.*

Surely this wasn't normal. Maybe it was some kind of post-divorce reaction? Perhaps, after almost a decade of struggling inside a failing marriage, she was finding Liam's attention just too exciting. The whole situation was getting out of hand. Their relationship was heating up way too quickly.

With this much fire, someone could get burned. And guess who it would be?

Not the boss!

She should be cooler and calmer about the whole thing. She wasn't a teenager. She was an adult in her thirties and she should be able to manage a relationship in a super-cool and controlled *adult* way—ultra-discreet at work and totally in control outside.

Taking a deep breath in and out, she scooped up her hair, gave it a little twist and used the butterfly clip from her top drawer to secure it away from her collar.

Not that it helped to make her feel any cooler or calmer. This was a fire that wouldn't be easy to tone down. Maybe she should speak to Liam. She could suggest they take things more slowly, talk more, rather than rushing straight into bed.

Right. Taking another deep breath, and with one

eye on Shana, she began to type a carefully worded, super-polite and admirably restrained reply to Liam's request.

'I've printed out these spreadsheets for you to look over,' the company accountant told Liam.

'Good, Merv; thank you.'

Merv began to set his work on Liam's desk and, as he did so, three emails appeared on Liam's computer screen. One was from Alice.

'They'll be fine,' Liam said a touch impatiently as Merv carefully made sure that each document was placed neatly and precisely and in exactly the right order.

'You might like to take a closer look at the projections for wages over the next six months, Mr Conway.'

'Yes, yes, sure.' Liam's eyes darted back to the screen.

'From these figures I'd suggest you consider leasing more of our IT equipment rather than owning it.'

Liam's hand hovered over the mouse, eager to click on Alice's response. 'I'll consider that. Yes, thank you, Merv.'

'And then there's the—'

'I'll give this report my thorough attention and then get back to you.'

At last Merv got the message. 'I'll leave it with you, then.'

Within a split-second of his turning to leave, Liam clicked on Alice's message.

If you could bring Indian curry and white wine, the

green plates will be ready and waiting. 6.30?
A.
P.S. I'll take care of dessert.
P.P.S. And the midnight snacks.
P.P.P.S. And breakfast.

Liam grinned. Maybe now he could stop the love-sick-teenager act and get back to running his business. Attending to this report from the Cairns accountant was only a small part of his duties.

His Sydney office coordinated a nationwide operation ranging from harbour tours and opera-house concerts to Kakadu tours and Snowy Mountains skiing holidays. If he was to succeed at making the Cairns business just as big and successful, it was time to focus, man. Focus.

He reached for his diary to check the calls he needed to make.

And at the same moment the telephone rang.

'Yes, Sally?'

'An urgent call's come through for you from Sydney, Mr Conway.'

'Thanks. I'll take it straight away.'

Rita James, his personal assistant in his head office in Sydney, was always super-calm and efficient, but today, just saying hello, she sounded worried.

'What's the problem, Rita?'

'I'm afraid there's bad news about Mrs Conway, Liam.'

Julia!

The news hit him with the force of a physical blow.

'Mrs Conway's housekeeper just rang to say that

she has been admitted to hospital and her condition's serious.'

Oh, God, no.

He'd been dreading something like this, had feared it might happen while he was away in the north.

'Do you have a phone number? Can I speak to Julia?'

'I'm afraid she isn't well enough to take calls.'

'Then I'll have to speak to the housekeeper. I don't know why Harriet didn't telephone me first. I gave her my new contact details.'

'Well, she was calling from the hospital and she sounded very upset. Perhaps she didn't have your Cairns number with her.'

'Whatever. It doesn't matter. I'll have to get on the first available plane.' He was struggling to stay calm. 'I assume there's someone responsible to take care of Jack?'

'I believe he's staying at the home of one of his school friends.'

'Right.' Liam's mind whirled. 'Do you have the details of the hospital? The ward?' Julia had to have the very best attention.

He jotted down the information Rita gave him.

'I'm sure she's in good hands,' she said, clearly trying to soothe him.

'Yes, I suppose you're right. Well, thanks for letting me know, Rita. I'll—no doubt, I'll see you soon.' Liam disconnected, ran his hands down his face and pressed his fingers against his eyelids. Hell!

This was not the first time Julia had been rushed to hospital, but that thought did nothing to ease his worry. It was always a nightmare.

Releasing a heart-rending sigh, he touched the button connecting him to Alice's extension.

'Alice, I'm sorry. I'm going to have to—'

'Alice isn't here.' It was Shana's voice.

'Oh.' Liam massaged his temple where an ache had started. 'Do you know where she is?'

'She took off in a hurry. Said something about emergency shopping.'

He sighed again. 'OK. When she comes back, tell her to call me.' Then he rang through to the front desk. 'Sally, can you book me on the first possible flight to Sydney? Yes, I want the next available flight. I *have* to be there tonight.'

Hot orange with pink polka dots.

Alice grinned at her reflection as she stood before the mirror in her new underwear. This fun ensemble should be a good test of Liam's liberal attitude to colour!

She'd bought it on the way home from work. Of course, she'd felt a little guilty about leaving early, but she knew she could make up for lost time tomorrow and the early mark seemed justified. After all, tonight was her first official date with Liam and surely that called for a quick detour via the shopping mall to buy scented candles.

Candlelight, wine, a leisurely meal and conversation were on the agenda for tonight. She and Liam needed to share more meaningful *verbal* exchanges, soulful heart-to-heart discussions. Until now she'd been reluctant to pressure him, but questions, like the ones Shana had raised, needed answers, as did others, like where their relationship might be heading.

Problem was, on the way to the candle shop she'd passed the lingerie shop, and she'd seen this cute bra and panties set in the window. The colours were so outrageous she immediately thought of Liam. And in spite of her commitment to being cool and calm and in control, she had rushed straight in and bought them.

And come home without the candles.

So much for being in control.

At least she had a sensible beige linen dress to wear over the fun lingerie. Alice slipped it on now and turned again to the mirror. This was better. The sleeveless shirtmaker dress was designed to be cool in the tropics, so it had very little shape, a stand-away collar and a row of sensible little buttons down the front.

Now she looked cool and, more importantly, modest.

Except…except…oh, how shameless could a girl get? All she wanted to think about was Liam's gorgeous, sexy smile when he undid these buttons and found what was *under* this modest beige dress.

Giving an exasperated shake, she hurried through to the kitchen and busied herself selecting plates, glassware, cutlery and place mats to set on the table out on her deck, *sans* candles. Halfway across the kitchen with her hands full, she heard her cell-phone ring. Darn. She'd left it in her bedroom and she had to put everything back on the kitchen counter while she went to answer it.

Please, don't let it be Mum or one of the aunts. Not tonight. Last night she'd spent ages on the phone, answering endless questions about the drama of the plane landing, and she'd had to explain that yes, Liam Conway was the same man her mother and aunts had seen in the photo in the paper and yes, it was an amazing coincidence that he'd turned out to be her boss. And yes, he was just as nice in real life as he'd appeared to be in the TV interviews.

The phone was on her bedside table.

'Hello, Alice.'

She could hardly hear Liam's voice above the buzz and hum of background noise—voices and busy, bustling sounds. She smiled as she pictured him waiting impatiently in the line-up at the crowded Indian take-away.

'Hi, Liam; is it going to be a long wait?'

'Alice, you didn't get my message to call me?'

She frowned. 'No.'

'Shana was supposed to tell you.'

'I—I—left work a little early.'

She heard his sigh. 'I'm sorry, Alice, I'm afraid I've had to cancel dinner. I'm at the airport now.'

'The airport?' Her heart gave an uncomfortable thud. 'What are you doing there?'

'Look, I'm terribly sorry, but something's come up and I have to fly to Sydney.'

'Tonight?' It was virtually impossible to keep the disappointment out of her voice.

'Yes. In fact the plane's boarding now.'

Whoosh. Alice's knees buckled. She dropped down onto her bed. This didn't make sense. What kind of *something* had come up?

'I'm really sorry,' Liam said again. 'When this news came through I was totally thrown. I've had so much on my mind this afternoon. There was a lot to get organised in a hurry.'

'What's happened?'

'It's—it's a family matter,' Liam told her. 'An emergency. It's too complicated to explain now. They're calling the final passengers for my flight. I'm going to have to turn this thing off.'

She was clutching the cell-phone so tightly it should have snapped in two. How could Liam just take off with so little warning, such scanty information?

'There's a chance I might have to stay in Sydney for some time,' he said. 'But I'll call you.'

'All right.' Her voice came out squeaky. *Some time.* How long was that?

'Are you OK?' He sounded concerned.

No, of course she wasn't okay. She was confused, disappointed, worried. Liam's evasions scared her. They were so horribly familiar. How many times had Todd rung just like this—at the last minute to make excuses?

What could Liam's emergency be? A dying parent? A road smash? Why was it complicated? Why couldn't he tell her? There was so much she didn't know about this man.

But she couldn't ask those questions now. 'Of course I'm fine,' she said. 'I'm sorry about—the emergency. I hope everything works out well.'

'Thanks. I'm going to miss you. Got to go. Bye.'

'I'll miss—' She didn't get a chance to finish the sentence. Liam had already disconnected.

She dropped the cell-phone onto her bedspread and sat in her darkened bedroom, numb with misery. She felt swamped by an irrational, unprecedented sadness and tears slipped down her cheeks.

Just like that, she'd plummeted from the heights of happiness to the depths of disappointment. She felt awful. Being in love just wasn't worth it. She'd felt empty and abandoned like this when she first suspected that Todd was cheating on her. How could she have found herself back in this ghastly place so quickly?

For several minutes she gave in to the wash of emotions, wallowing in self-pity. This wasn't fair. How could Liam be so offhand with her? He wasn't like Todd, was he? She couldn't bear it if he was.

But eventually she pressed her knuckles to her streaming eyes and drew a deep breath. OK. She had to get a grip. After all, she was trying to handle this relationship like a mature adult and it was downright silly to fall in a heap over one broken date.

Liam was dealing with what must be a very serious family emergency and she was crying like a spoilt child who couldn't go out to play because it was raining.

Using her hands to lever herself up from the mattress, she stood and went through to the bathroom, where she washed her face, and then she went into the kitchen to make something to eat—a grilled cheese sandwich and coffee.

As she slapped sliced cheese onto bread, she decided that she should be grateful for this timely lesson. After her divorce she'd been determined to join the single-and-loving-it brigade. She'd vowed that she wasn't going to rely on another person to make her happy or to give meaning to her life.

And what had she done? She'd let a man become the centre of her life again.

She hadn't learned a thing from her divorce.

Her first waking thoughts were for Liam, and so were far too many of her thoughts during the hours in between. And she drifted to sleep thinking of him.

In other words she'd fallen head over heels in love, which was just plain foolish. Thirty-year-old women just didn't fall in love with their bosses and dream of happily-ever-after. They had flings. That was what she'd had. A fling. Sex, not love.

There'd been lots and lots of fabulous passion but no talk of love, no promises, no talk of the future at all. For all Alice knew, Liam could have a girlfriend in Sydney. And, as a contemporary, liberated, New Age woman, she shouldn't mind.

Ouch.

Hot melted cheese dripped onto her hand and she grabbed for a dishcloth to mop it, and felt the threat of tears again. Darn it. She knew that she *would* mind. She would mind very much if Liam had another girlfriend.

Oh, good grief, she'd be bitterly disappointed. Devastated.

CHAPTER SEVEN

'THEY haven't changed the date of Valentine's Day, have they?'

Alice was in the middle of a phone call when she looked up to see Sally, the front-desk receptionist, walking through the doorway bearing a huge bouquet of red roses.

Walking straight to Alice, Sally winked and set the flowers on her desk with a cheeky *ta-da!* flourish.

Alice's heart began to knock and she lost the train of her conversation with a hire-car rep in Mount Isa.

Who on earth would be sending her flowers? They had to be from Liam. But would he make such a public gesture at work?

Smiling broadly, Sally tapped her fingernail against the little envelope that was pinned to red satin ribbons.

Alice knew she was blushing as she mouthed 'thank you' and she was grateful that her phone call meant that Sally couldn't hang around while the envelope was opened. But just as the call finished, Shana walked in. *Great.*

'Wow! Who sent you these?'

'I've no idea.' Alice tried very hard to sound cool as Shana fingered the envelope.

'Aren't you going to have a look?'

'Of course.' Darn. Her fingers were shaking as she struggled to pull out the tiny pin that secured the card.

'I'll bet they're from the boss. Things are hotting up, aren't they?' Shana leaned close with a forced enthusiasm that did nothing to calm Alice.

Her fingers fumbled with the seal on the envelope. She hadn't heard from Liam since he'd dashed off to Sydney. These flowers must be from him. There was no other man in her life and no other explanation. She was going to be floating on happiness for days.

She read the card and blinked.

'Well?' Shana's cry was close to a squeal. 'Come on, Alice, spill.'

'They're from Joe,' she said, trying hard not to sound disappointed.

'Joe? Who's Joe?'

'The pilot who collapsed in the plane.'

'Oh.' Shana couldn't wipe the relieved smirk from her face. 'How nice.'

'Yes. It's a very sweet note. He's completely recovered now and he thinks I saved his life.'

'I'm sure you did.' Shana gave Alice a pat-you-on-the-head smile and continued on to her desk.

Disappointment deluged Alice. She had so wanted these lovely flowers to be a gift from Liam. What was he doing in Sydney? Why had he cut her off?

Mad with herself that it mattered so much, she returned her attention to Joe's card. His message really was sweet. He claimed he'd been brought back to life by the kiss of an angel. Who else could it have been at that altitude? he'd asked.

And then, further down, she saw another message in different writing:

Alice, we want to thank you sincerely from the bot-

tom of our hearts for saving Joe's life. He is a
precious husband and father and we still have him,
thanks to you and Mr Conway.

Jean, Gary, Jenny and Jana Banyo

Alice touched a dark, velvety rose petal. At the
time she'd helped Joe she hadn't given a thought to
his wife and children. She'd just done what had to be
done. But everyone had families. Even the simplest
action could have wide-reaching effects.

The flowers were a lovely gesture and, as she got
on with her work, she tried to convince herself that
she'd rather receive an uplifting message from Joe
and his family than a bunch of flowers from her remote and aloof boss.

But by the end of the week the flowers were wilted
and so were Alice's spirits. She still hadn't heard anything from Liam.

He left a brief message with Sally, to say that he
hoped to be back the following Monday. But that was
all.

Of course, everyone in the office expected Alice to
be able to supply them with details about what the
boss was doing in Sydney. And it was anything but
pleasant to admit that she was more or less as clueless
as they were.

It was all very difficult—embarrassing—and confusing.

One minute she was angry. Why was it so darned
hard for Liam to call her? And then the next she
would wonder if she was expecting too much of him.
If only she wasn't so unsure of her role in his life.

She was unsure of everything. Todd had made her

so insecure. And his legacy was that she didn't really know what she wanted now: she didn't want a new relationship, and yet she wanted Liam.

Dennis had a field-day in the boss's absence. 'What's with this fellow?' he cried. 'He flies up here, insists on having hands-on involvement, goes through our entire operation with a fine-tooth comb to the point where we're virtually having fingernail inspections, and then he rushes off again.' He shot a suspicious glance Alice's way. 'Is this some kind of test?'

'No, of course not, it's a family emergency.' Oh, dear. How unfortunately vague that sounded.

'A family emergency?' Shana repeated, never missing the chance to gossip. 'So his wife's found out that Liam's straying, has she?'

She smiled too sweetly at Alice, who had no answer other than to shoot her a drop-dead look.

Liam stared at the famous Sydney skyline.

Once upon a time this office, with its stunning views, had been the pinnacle of his ambition. Now, as he surveyed the glorious harbour, the spectacular opera house and the unique coat-hanger bridge, he found little in this high-status vista to comfort him.

What a dreadful week it had been!

Emotionally he was exhausted. He'd been to hell and back during his long vigil at the hospital. But at last Julia was out of the woods. In a few days she would be going home again. In another week she would be more or less back to normal, or as normal as she could ever be.

Not that Julia considered her life to be anything

less than normal. Her endurance of hardship was amazing. She never complained and was always smiling.

It was Liam who had never come to terms with seeing her in a wheelchair. She managed beautifully, but he could never forget how lovely and lithe and full of life she had been before the accident.

He hadn't allowed himself to think about Alice this week. The contrast between her passionate vitality and Julia's weakness was too cruel, his sense of guilt too sharply painful.

'Liam.'

He turned at the sound of his PA's voice.

'Mr Toh is here.'

'Already?' Liam glanced at his wrist-watch and sighed. 'Very well. Tell him I'll be with him in a minute.'

Time to snap his brain back into corporate mode.

Kenny Toh, a Singaporean businessman, headed Asia-Pacific Investments and potentially he was a major financial partner in Kanga Tours. API was proposing to fund vital expansion of their business and when Kenny had heard that Liam was in Sydney he flew in from Singapore to meet Liam, to talk to him face to face, to view his product, and to generally size him up.

He would expect to be taken on a tour of the city, wined and dined, introduced around. The process couldn't be hurried or dismissed lightly and would probably take several days.

Liam knew he shouldn't feel trapped by the fellow. In the past he'd found international networking to be the aspect of his business he enjoyed most. But now it kept him from getting back to Cairns.

To Alice.

'Rita,' Liam called as his assistant was almost out of the room. 'One other thing. Could you please telephone the Cairns office?'

'Certainly.'

'I'd like to pass a private message to…' He paused and then swore softly. No, he didn't want Rita to ring Alice at the office. Scowling angrily, he rubbed at his forehead. He hadn't spoken to Alice in a week.

There was no time to ring her now.

Suddenly he gave an abrupt little laugh of triumph as he hit on a better idea. 'Can you take time to do some shopping today?'

'Well, yes. What would you like me to get you?'

When Liam told her what he wanted and where he wanted it sent, Rita's eyebrows lifted high, but then, like a well-trained PA, she lowered them again just as quickly. 'I can do that in my lunch break,' she said.

'Take as long as you need,' Liam told her and then he grabbed his suit jacket from its peg near the door and shrugged it on as he went out to greet Mr Toh.

Alice had never been so glad to reach the end of the working week.

Friday afternoon. She could scurry home and hide.

She could be pathetic and lonely and no one would notice.

Keeping up appearances in the office, pretending a nonchalance she didn't feel, had nearly killed her, but now she could stop pretending that she didn't care what Liam was doing in Sydney, who he was with, or that he hadn't contacted her. She'd suffered two weeks of sleepless nights and stressful days—no wonder she felt tired, weepy and sick in the stomach whenever she thought about food.

As she parked her car in the garage, she wondered if she should try to drag herself out somewhere tonight, to a movie perhaps. If she really exhausted herself she might sleep at last. She should make an effort to do *something*.

She grabbed her briefcase from the passenger seat, locked the car and went to check the mailbox. Two envelopes with windows. Nothing personal, just bills. Terrific.

She was halfway up the path to her front door when a van pulled up, a courier express-delivery van, and the driver was looking directly at her.

Intensely curious, she waited and watched him get out, extract a largish parcel from the back of the van and begin to walk towards her.

'I have a delivery for—' he squinted to read the name on the address '—Alice Madigan.'

'That's me,' she said and she realised she was trembling. How silly, but she'd seen a Sydney postmark.

Her heart kept up a wild kind of skipping as she signed for the parcel, thanked the delivery man and carried the box into the house. She set it on the kitchen counter and found a sharp knife to cut through the tape, and she seemed to take ages to undo the packaging and the masses of bubble wrap, but at last the contents were revealed.

A beautiful glass bowl. It was gorgeous. A wave of shimmering ocean-green was magically suspended within curved, clear glass. Holding it up to the light, she was overawed by its beauty and craftsmanship. It had to have been terribly expensive.

A little card inside explained that the glass was hand-blown by artisans from Murano, which she knew was a famous island off the coast of Venice. She searched for a signature, turned the card over and found a message carefully printed in black ink. *Missing you like crazy.*

Oh, wow.

She felt a wave of giddiness, or was that happiness? Carefully she set the bowl on the counter.

Liam.

Liam was missing her.

How fantastic. But how confusing, too. How could he take the time to go shopping for a gift when he didn't have time to phone her?

No. She wasn't going to over-analyse this. Liam was thinking of her and he'd sent her a beautiful gift. Just because he'd been gone for...

Feeling a sudden need to count the days, she looked up at the calendar on her kitchen wall and then she frowned.

No.

She must be mistaken. Leaning closer, she studied the dates more carefully, flipped back to the red dot marked on the previous month and counted forward again.

That was odd. Her period had been due three days ago. She'd been so distracted she hadn't noticed. But she must have miscalculated. Perhaps she'd marked the wrong day last month. She was never late. She knew *that* for sure. She'd spent years watching and waiting and her body was like clockwork. Never once had she been more than a day late.

She was quite confident that her period was on its way. She had all the usual premenstrual symptoms. In fact, she'd been more tired and tender and stressed-out than ever this week.

She looked again at the bowl—so beautiful and vivid, as if a living piece of ocean had been captured and imprisoned in glass.

How silly she'd been to fuss about Liam's absence. No doubt the stress had thrown her hormones out of whack. Now she could calm down.

What she needed was an early night. She would wake up in the morning and her period would arrive and her life would carry on in its usual, predictable rhythm.

CHAPTER EIGHT

THE woman in the chemist shop smiled at Alice. 'This is our most popular brand. It comes with instructions. One blue line means a negative result, two lines positive. And you get two testing kits.'

'Two?' Alice repeated with a gulp.

'Some people like to double-check.'

'Yes. Right. Thanks, I'll take it.'

Clutching the packet to her chest, Alice hurried outside and almost jumped into her car. Then she opened the packet, took out the box and sat for several minutes staring at the printed words: *Pregnancy Test*.

She couldn't believe this was happening to her. Her period couldn't really be five days overdue.

Except…she'd checked the calendar and her diary a thousand times this weekend. And every time she'd arrived at the same answer. So here she was on Sunday night, so unable to bear the suspense any longer that she'd rushed out to find a 24-hour pharmacy.

She felt a bit silly really, testing when she knew the kit was going to show one blue line, a negative result. She couldn't be pregnant. It simply wasn't possible. Todd had been desperate for a son and they'd tried for almost two years with no luck.

His doctor had run tests on him that proved without a doubt that it was her fault. She shuddered now just remembering Todd's anger and the ghastly names he'd called her. He'd made her feel so useless, so unfeminine and unlovable; her self-esteem had hit rock bottom.

By the time he'd finished abusing her, she'd accepted the blame, of course. Why wouldn't it be her fault? She'd let him down in every other way.

She realised now that she should have double-checked Todd's assertion with fertility tests of her own, but at the time she hadn't been able to face going through painful medical procedures just to confirm something she already knew.

Besides, what was the point? Almost immediately, Todd had turned to other women.

Setting the box carefully on the seat beside her, she started the car and drove home through the quiet suburban traffic. It was raining. Tyres swished through puddles and headlights slanted across shiny roads. Even though she knew it was pointless, she couldn't suppress a tiny kernel of crazy excitement. But it felt so unreal. This couldn't be an ordinary Sunday night, with families at home watching television and wishing the weekend could last a little longer.

By the time she reached home she was a bundle of nerves, but it was time to put an end to the awful tension that had made a nightmare of her weekend. With the test over and done with she could go to work tomorrow confident that at least one potential problem had been overruled.

OK.

She set the testing stick on the bathroom bench, sat on the edge of the bath tub and closed her eyes while she counted the minutes.

All weekend she'd felt as if she were teetering on a knife edge, on the brink of toppling into someone else's life, some weird other dimension, like Alice falling into Wonderland. Very soon now and her own life would rock back into place.

Once she knew for sure that she was right, that she wasn't pregnant, she could —

Oh, my God. She leapt to her feet.

There were two of them.

Two blue lines.

Trembling, she stared at the tiny window on the testing stick. Good heavens. Sinking back onto the edge of the bath tub, she tried to take it in.

She was pregnant.

No, it must be a mistake.

Heart pounding, she rushed back to the kitchen to grab the second kit. It had to be an error. The woman in the chemist shop said people liked to double-check. That was probably because the first test was often wrong.

She felt shaky and sick with a weird kind of excitement as she stood staring again at another tiny plastic window, watching the first line form and then, oh good grief, the second one.

Oh, heavens. Oh, Liam.

What have I done?

In a daze she wandered through her flat, trying to take it in. The test said she was pregnant. Her period hadn't come and her breasts felt unusually tight and tender. Her body said she was pregnant.

It didn't make sense.

*   *   *

'I don't understand. How could it have happened?' she asked the doctor next evening.

He looked at her with amused surprise. 'You don't really need me to explain about the birds and the bees, do you, Alice?'

'No, of course not. But I'm supposed to be infertile.'

The doctor frowned and then glanced back at his computer screen, scrolling through her records.

'You won't find anything there. I didn't actually have any medical tests,' she admitted.

'Well, my dear, if there was a problem, it seems that nature has taken care of it. You can go home and tell your husband the good news that you're not infertile any more.'

'Yes,' she said softly.

There was only one answer, she thought as she drove home. Todd had lied to her. As soon as she had slept with another man she'd fallen pregnant, which meant that Todd's stubborn macho pride must have prevented him from admitting that he was the one who was sterile.

Or perhaps he'd never had the test and had simply convinced himself that it must be her problem. The silly sod. Had he chased other women in a desperate bid to prove his virility, his fertility?

For a brief moment she almost felt sorry for him, but then she was too busy feeling sorry for herself. How dared Todd lie? Damn him. She would never have taken a risk with Liam if she'd thought there was any chance of pregnancy.

She was a mess of whirlwind emotions. One minute angry, the next scared and then, in the next breath, incredibly happy.

There was a baby growing inside her.

She almost smiled at the careful way she walked from her garage to the front door with a hand cradling her abdomen, as if she was a fragile vessel with sacred cargo. It was amazing and scary to think of a tiny baby alive and growing in her womb. Her baby.

It was a fantasy she'd never allowed herself.

She gave in to it now—saw herself in a few months' time in snazzy maternity dress, proud of her round pregnant stomach. She envisioned a divine little nursery, with a white bassinette and delicate baby things—special little soaps and baby talcum powder and little pots of baby lotions.

She could almost imagine her mother and aunts knitting or crocheting tiny things…

And Liam. Where was he in this picture?

She tried to picture him standing beside her, tall and proud, with a protective arm about her shoulders, and a look of loving wonder in his eyes.

And then, of course, the foolish picture fractured. She had no idea how Liam would react to her news. She'd insisted she was safe, that she couldn't possibly get pregnant, and he'd trusted her completely.

The only communication she'd had since he left was the brief message that had accompanied the beautiful green glass bowl. He'd been away so long he almost felt like a stranger.

Sinking onto a lounge chair, she wrapped her arms across her middle. Liam wasn't a family man. If he was he'd have married years ago. He was a businessman, a high flier. When he learned that she was pregnant he might well decide she'd been trying to trap him and he would have every right to be angry with her.

What a mess she was in. There was every chance that Liam would be furious. And there was no way her mother and aunts were going to leap into action to knit baby clothes. They would be too outraged by the shock and shame Alice had foisted yet again on her family.

As for everyone at work—damn—how could she face them?

She felt so overwhelmed she couldn't cry. This was like the nightmare of her divorce all over again.

The bad times were supposed to be behind her. She'd met Liam in the Hippo Bar on her thirtieth birthday as a contemporary, liberated, single woman—and what had happened?

She'd fallen into the same trap that had been ensnaring women since time began.

Monday morning brought worse news.

Dennis's eyes were almost popping out of his head. 'You're never going to believe this,' he said, staring directly at Alice.

'What?' cried all three women at once, and poor Alice's heart took off like a sky rocket.

Dennis wet his lips and took a dramatic deep breath. 'The boss is back and he's brought his wife with him.'

'He's what?'

'He can't have.'

This time the chorus of cries was closer to shrieks.

A wave of nausea rose into Alice's throat and she felt so suddenly awful she thought she might faint.

'Mr Conway can't be married,' said Mary-Ann, sending anxious looks to Alice.

'I'm sorry but you're wrong,' said Dennis airily. 'He's turned up with a woman and her name is Mrs Conway and he was paying her a great deal of attention when he lifted her out of the limo a moment ago.'

'Lifted her?' cried Shana, leaping from her seat and tearing across the room to peer through the slats of the venetian blind that screened their office from the front reception area. 'Oh, my God.' Her eyes were as huge as Dennis's as she turned back to Alice. 'She's in a wheelchair.'

Alice was glued to her seat.

'Come and look,' hissed Shana.

No, Alice didn't want to. She couldn't.

Dennis was at the window with Shana now and they were both riveted by the scene taking place in the foyer.

'I wonder who the young fellow is,' mused Dennis. 'Their son?'

A son? Could this get any worse? Alice's heart pounded like a battering ram; her stomach lurched. Liam couldn't have a wife. He couldn't; he couldn't. He'd told her he wasn't married. She believed him.

By now Mary-Ann was at the window too. 'Gosh, she's beautiful,' she said in a low, rather awestruck voice.

Both women turned back to Alice.

'Come and have a look,' said Shana again.

Alice's legs felt leaden as she struggled to her feet. For a horrible moment she thought *she* might need a wheelchair just to get across the room, but somehow she made it. Shana had adjusted the blinds so it was possible to look out without being observed.

She looked and saw Liam out in the foyer with a woman in a wheelchair and a boy of about fifteen. Liam's hands were resting on the back of the chair and he was smiling and talking to Sally at the front desk. The woman in the chair was laughing.

Shana was right; Mrs Conway was beautiful. She had delicate features, high cheekbones and long autumn-coloured, wavy hair. She was smartly dressed in a cream silk blouse with a chic scarf in mocha tones draped with casual elegance over her shoulders. A longish dark olive-green skirt covered her legs.

There was something very appealing about her, a kind of inner light and friendly warmth. Under other circumstances Alice suspected that she might like the woman very much.

The boy was tall, with the typically gangly build of a teenager, and he had dark hair like Liam's.

As she and her workmates hovered at the window, spying on them, the trio began to move away, down the corridor towards the accountant's office. Alice swayed on her feet. Any minute now she was going to be sick. Or she was going to faint. She wasn't sure which.

Dennis snatched up the nearest phone. 'Sally,' he hissed to the girl just a few feet away from them in Reception. 'What's going on? What's the boss up to?'

The three women watched in tense silence as he received the answers. His eyes flashed mysteriously as he hung up.

'Come on, then,' cried Shana. 'Put us out of our misery.'

'Well,' said Dennis slowly, enjoying the power of his secret, 'her name is Mrs Julia Conway and she's moved here from Sydney. She plans to live here and the boss is going in to talk to Merv, because he's buying her a house.'

A house! Alice was swamped by a wave of shock. That could only mean... Surely that meant the woman must be...

With a hand clasped over her mouth, she bolted for the corridor, heading in the direction of the Ladies'.

'Liam, what's the matter with you?' asked Julia Conway. 'You've been pacing about like a caged lion all evening.'

Liam paused midway down the length of the balcony that opened off his apartment's living room. 'I'm sorry,' he said. 'I've been a little distracted.'

'More than a little.' Julia laughed gently. 'I doubt you've heard a word I've said in the past fifteen minutes.'

'Have I been that rude? Sorry.'

'Who is she?'

His jaw dropped. Julia's blunt question had caught him completely off guard.

She laughed again. 'I'm right. I knew it was something personal. You're never like this when it's work. If you were worried about a business matter you'd be on the phone, getting to the bottom of the problem.'

He lowered himself into a wicker chair beside her and shoved his hands deep in his trouser pockets. 'Am I really that transparent?'

'To me you are, but then I've known you for nearly twenty years. And you're so like Jack. He has a hard time keeping secrets from me too.'

The sound of taped laughter floated out from the living room, where Jack was watching television.

For a little while they sat in companionable silence.

'What a deliciously balmy night this is,' Julia said. 'I know this tropical climate is going to be wonderful for me.' She laid a cool hand on Liam's arm. 'Thank you so much. For everything.'

They shared a smile and then Julia gave his wrist a playful slap. 'Now, why don't you hop on the phone and talk to this woman? Put your mind at rest. Where is she? In Sydney?'

'Actually, no, she's here in Cairns.'

Julia's eyes widened. 'That was quick. You were only here for a week or so before I threw a spanner in the works with my dash to hospital.'

'Yeah.' His shoulders lifted in a brief shrug. 'It was kind of spontaneous.'

'Spontaneous? How unlike you, Liam.' Her eyes sparkled. 'I really like the sound of this.'

'It's nothing serious,' Liam insisted when he saw the hope that flared in her eyes.

Liar. His right hand closed around the little jewellery box in his pocket.

In an act of complete spontaneity—or insanity—he'd bought a ring in Sydney…an emerald, of course. It had been a totally off-the-wall, spur-of-the-moment impulse, fuelled by a whim of fierce sentiment, and Liam still couldn't quite believe he'd done it. He knew it was reckless and impulsive.

But it hadn't felt foolish.

Not at the time.

Now, however, he realised just how rash he'd been. There were difficult bridges to cross before he asked a woman to share his life. He would have to reveal the shadows that stalked him.

Beside him, Julia let out a worried sigh. 'Liam, don't look so gruff. I didn't mean to sound as if I was criticising you just now. I'm all for spontaneity. You know I'd be only too delighted to see you indulge in a little romance. It would be better still if you fell completely head over heels in love.'

He smiled at her. 'You've been pushing me at other women for years.'

'With very little success.' After a bit Julia said, 'I hope you haven't stayed in this evening to keep me company.'

'It's your first night in town. You've been ill. I'm certainly not going to desert you.'

'I'm absolutely fine now.' She glanced at her wrist-watch. 'It's not very late. Why don't you go out? I'll watch a little television with Jack. I'd like an early night.'

Liam nodded, but he didn't move. He sat staring out across the dark, moonlit water of Trinity Inlet, thinking about Alice, worrying about her. She was ill apparently and she'd gone home from work mid-morning, but she hadn't answered his calls. He'd left three messages on her answering machine and she hadn't returned any of them. And yet her workmates were almost certain that she was at home, which meant she was either too sick to answer the phone— or she was avoiding him.

Either way he was worried.

Movement beside him dragged him out of his dark thoughts. Julia had turned her wheelchair and was heading back inside. He leapt to his feet.

'Shoo, Liam,' she said, waving a hand over her shoulder. And then she dropped her head back and winked up at him. 'I mean that in the nicest possible way, of course.'

Bending down, he dropped a quick kiss on her cheek. 'All right, if you insist, I'll go.'

She continued inside, while he flipped open his cell-phone and called for a taxi. And then he went downstairs and waited on the footpath for the cab to arrive.

The night was indeed, as Julia had said, balmy. He drew a deep breath and caught a whiff of salt from the sea as well as perfume from a nearby garden, a very sweet, heady, floral fragrance. The deep breath didn't calm him. In fact, he was astonished by how nervous he felt. By the way his heart was pumping anyone would think Alice Madigan was armed and dangerous.

But of course…she was armed…with a dangerously sensual femininity that had made him her captive slave.

This evening, however, when she opened her front door and saw Liam on her doorstep, all colour drained from her face.

'Oh,' was all she said and she clutched the door knob as if she needed its support.

'Hello, Alice.' He was alarmed by her apparent frailty. 'I hope I haven't got you out of bed.'

'No, no.'

Despite her paleness, her beauty couldn't be dimmed. Her dark hair was shining as if she'd just finished brushing it a thousand times and her deep red jeans and multi-toned T-shirt offset her pale skin perfectly. He wanted to feast his eyes on her. 'I was very sorry to hear that you weren't well.'

She nodded, but offered no explanation.

'It's nothing serious, I hope?'

'No. Just a stomach virus.' She gave a little shrug, but its effect was rather spoiled by the bleakness in her eyes that suggested she was troubled by much more than a stomach bug. 'You must think I make a habit of leaving work early.'

'Not at all.' Liam stood on the step with his hands shoved deep in his pockets and she continued to cling to the door. 'May I come in?' he asked and then, reluctantly, 'Or are you too tired?'

'I—I'm rather tired.'

The tension between them was palpable. He couldn't stand it. Taking a step closer, he reached out and touched her cheek. It was soft and warm beneath his fingers. 'I've missed you so much, Alice.'

She turned her head away quickly, but not before he saw the movement of her throat as she swallowed and the sudden glitter of silver in her eyes. Were they tears? What was the matter? His heart rocked.

Standing stiffly, with his hand returned to his side, he struggled to think of something else to say. This stilted conversation was agony, but it was an agony that had to be prolonged. He couldn't walk away till he knew what the matter was. 'I hope my parcel arrived safely.'

'Oh, yes. I meant to thank you.' She looked up at

him again. 'I've never had any Venetian glass. It's just gorgeous. I love it.'

'You found a place for it among all your other green things?'

'Yes.' She cast a quick glance over her shoulder and he thought for a moment that she was going to invite him inside to see it, but obviously she dismissed that idea almost as quickly as it had come to her and she gave the door a little push as if she was keen to shut him out.

'I assume everything went smoothly in the office while I was away.' He was grasping at straws now.

One corner of her mouth tilted in a wry smile. 'We managed very well without you.'

Her deliberate taunt found its mark. He sighed. 'I guess you're angry because I didn't make contact while I was away.'

She didn't reply—just stood there looking upset

'I'm sorry I haven't been in touch,' he said. 'It was a little crazy in Sydney.'

She dropped her gaze quickly. Her feet were bare and she rubbed one nervously against the other.

'Is it something else? What is it, Alice? What's the matter?'

Her mouth tugged out of shape and then a little sound that was suspiciously like a sob escaped. 'Just about everything.'

Hearing that, Liam gave up waiting for an invitation. He pushed the door out of her grasp and stepped inside.

There wasn't much room in the narrow hallway and in the confined space he was acutely aware of her proximity. The scent of lemon shampoo lingered about her and he wanted to ignore whatever was bothering her and to draw her close, to have her in his arms, with her warm, sweet body rammed tight against him, to bury his face in her fragrant, silky hair.

But he continued walking down the hallway and turned into her living room, and she closed the front door and followed.

Her living room was almost in darkness save for the gentle glow cast by a table lamp in the far corner. It was a room of intense atmosphere with strong pieces of furniture, richly coloured wall hangings, cleverly selected cushions and *objets d'art*. There was music playing softly—a woman singing a moody love song about walking in fields of gold.

The urge to drag Alice down onto the deep chocolate sofa was so strong Liam almost groaned aloud.

'Now,' he said gruffly as he stood to attention in the middle of her room. 'You're going to tell me what's the matter.'

A look of despair swept over her lovely face.

'And you'll also tell me how I can help,' he added more gently.

She shook her head. 'I don't want your help.'

The hardness in her voice caused an involuntary flinch, but he chose to ignore it. 'Take a seat, Alice.' He said this as he might have done to an employee in his office and he half expected an angry response, but she sat meekly in a deep armchair and he took the sofa.

They faced each other in the lamplight.

'So, what kind of problem are we dealing with here?' He was aware that he sounded more like a boss at a board meeting than a lover.

The wry smile returned, tilting her soft pink mouth to an unhappy slant. 'On a scale of one to ten?'

'If that's the way you want to present it.'

Picking up a cocoa and black striped cushion, she hugged it to her chest and sighed. 'From my point of view, right at this moment, it feels like a ten.'

'Good God, Alice, is it that bad?' A knife point twisted in his heart. 'You're not seriously ill, are you?'

'No,' she said quickly, but then she dropped the cushion as she covered her face with her hands.

'What is it?' Liam was across the floor and kneeling beside her. He couldn't bear this. His heart filled his throat.

She dragged her hands slowly down her face and her eyes glittered again with the hint of silver. 'I'm really embarrassed about this,' she said.

'What?' he demanded in a breathless gasp.

'I—I'm—' She swallowed and a tear spilled down her cheek. 'I'm pregnant.'

It was as if she'd thrown a grenade in his face. He felt strangely numb. He knew there was a reason why her words didn't make sense, but for the moment he couldn't think of it, couldn't think at all.

And then slowly the shock subsided.

'When? How?'

'The outback trip is the only time it could have happened. I'm sorry,' Alice said. 'I had no idea.'

Sinking onto the carpeted floor with his hands behind him for support, he let his thoughts unscramble. 'You said pregnancy was impossible.'

'I know. I thought I was infertile. Honestly.' Her hands were clenched tightly on her knees. 'Apparently, I was mistaken.' She looked directly at him. 'You have a right to be angry.' Her eyes were the colour of rainwater and awash with tears. 'You are angry, aren't you?'

CHAPTER NINE

ALL Alice wanted was to hurl herself into Liam's arms. Here he was, returned to her, in her house again after the long days of waiting, and she yearned to feel him holding her. But how could she, now that she'd seen his wife? And how could she when the impact of her bombshell was ricocheting through him like shockwaves?

He was sinking back onto the floor, completely stunned, but then, as she watched through tear-blurred eyes, he leapt to his feet and strode away from her, one hand rubbing the back of his neck as he wrestled with her news.

When he turned back to her, his eyes were burning with a fierce blue light and his throat muscles betrayed a terrible tension.

'I know you must think I tricked you,' she said in a shaking voice. 'But I can assure you I honestly believed I couldn't have a baby.' When he didn't reply she hurried on. 'I don't want this to be your concern, Liam. It's my problem, and I will deal with it. You don't have to worry that I'll make unreasonable demands or anything.'

His eyes speared her. 'What do you mean, you'll deal with it? You're not thinking of a termination, are you?'

'Heavens, no. I just mean I'll manage on my own. I don't need—'

'Me?' His hands clenched tightly against his sides and his face flushed dark red. Corded sinews stood out on his forearms. 'Is that what you're saying, Alice? You don't need me? You don't want me involved?'

No. I need you, Liam. I need your arms about me. I need the touch of your lips on mine, on me, anywhere, everywhere.

'I—I don't want you to feel under any obligation,' she said.

'And you would reject an offer of marriage?'

Marriage? A jolt, like an electric shock, scorched through her. An offer of marriage was the very last thing she'd expected to hear from this man. It wasn't possible.

She'd thought he might offer her money…or friendship…even a long-term affair. 'You—you can't mean that.'

His face was so stiff and proud it might well have been cast in bronze. 'Why not?'

'You're not available.'

He frowned. 'What the hell are you talking about?'

At first she thought she might not get the words out but somehow she managed. 'Your wife.'

'My what?' He released a short, disbelieving huff that might have been a laugh. 'What are you on about? I'm not married, Alice. I've never been married. I told you that.'

She pressed a hand against the savage beating wings in her chest. 'Mrs Conway, the woman who arrived with you today—'

'Julia? She's not my wife. She's my sister-in-law.'

She stared at him, saw naked emotion in his eyes

and knew that he was telling the truth. A sister-in-law. Why hadn't she thought of that? 'W-was she the family emergency?'

'Yes. Julia's been in hospital. Unfortunately, she has to deal with medical complications that crop up from time to time.'

Now that she was adjusting to this news, anger began to surface. 'It might have helped if you'd telephoned.'

'Yes.' With his hands on his hips Liam stared at the far wall. 'I can see now that it was a mistake to wait, but I thought it would be wiser to explain it all when I got back. For heaven's sake, Alice, I told you I wasn't married. Couldn't you believe me? Why would I lie?'

'I don't know.' Her hands flapped at her sides as she struggled to justify why she'd doubted him.

'Men lie. For all sorts of reasons.'

'That's a wild generalisation.'

'Todd lied to me. He told me he'd had medical tests that proved our fertility problems were my fault.'

Liam muttered an oath. 'I'd appreciate it if you didn't draw parallels between me and that toad.'

'You're nothing like him,' Alice said softly. She drew a deep breath. 'Mrs Conway—your sister-in-law—I only caught a glimpse of her, but I thought she looked rather nice.'

'She is. Julia's wonderful.'

'And she's married to your brother?'

'My brother's dead.' This was uttered with such jaw-clenched finality that Alice accepted it without daring to comment.

But then Liam's face broke into a heartbreakingly

sad smile. 'This isn't how tonight should be happening, Alice. I feel so—so distanced from you. It feels like we're fighting.'

'I don't want to fight,' she whispered, her eyes brimming.

In two steps Liam was beside her again and the next moment he was scooping her up and a beat later he was in her armchair and she was in his lap and his arms were about her and she was clinging to him.

Hooking a strand of hair with his finger, he tucked it behind her ear. His warm lips caressed her cheek. 'We've made a baby together, Alice. It's a night for celebration.'

'Celebration?'

'As I remember, we're rather good at it.'

'But it's what got us into this trouble.'

'We're not in trouble.'

Perhaps he was right. Besides, she couldn't resist his kiss. And he gave her little option. His mouth claimed her, calmed her. With her eyes closed she relaxed into him and it was perfect—a deliciously sensual and unhurried kiss, different from the passion and fire of their kisses in the past.

There was a tenderness, a loving lingering, as if they both felt just a little overawed by the astonishing, deeper connection of impending parenthood.

When at last they broke apart, Liam buried his face in her hair. 'Even without a baby in the picture, whatever has happened between us is more than just sex, Alice.'

'I know,' she whispered.

His lips brushed her ear. 'I think you should marry me.'

Marriage. Alice went very still in his arms.

Here it was again; another proposal. Every part of her wanted Liam. But marriage? Could she make a commitment like that? So soon?

It was so tempting, but was it just an easy way to avoid the problems of pregnancy out of wedlock?

She knew she was madly attracted to this man— almost certainly in love with him. But how could she be sure it wasn't for all the wrong reasons? Liam Conway was powerful and rich, a sensational lover and oh, so divine looking—in other words, every woman's dream.

But did she know the real man?

At sixteen, Todd had been the epitome of most high-school girls' dreams and she'd fallen for the whole gorgeous-footballer thing. But when she got to know Todd inside the harsh day-to-day realities of married life there had been so many disappointments. Those disappointments had created little rifts at first, but over time the gaps had widened and deepened until the damage was irreparable.

One failed marriage had been a nightmare; another would be more than she could bear.

Liam was waiting for her answer. She could feel the tension in his arms as he sensed her struggle. She closed her eyes, wishing this wasn't so hard.

'It's too soon, isn't it?' he said.

A little sigh of relief escaped her. He understood. She nodded against his shoulder, but then she lifted her head. 'That's not the only reason.'

'You have a string of reasons for rejecting me?'

It was impossible to discuss this while she was

curled on his lap. She hoisted herself onto her feet and stood facing him.

It was time to be sensible.

'You know I've just ended one marriage, Liam. I'm not ready to dive into another.'

He nodded slowly, his eyes stern, his reactions unreadable.

'And, as I said before, I wouldn't want you to marry me just because you feel obliged to.'

Liam's jaw tightened and he flicked his gaze away from her to a woven hanging of rainforest trees and palms on her far wall.

'In many ways you're still a stranger,' she said, glad that he wasn't looking her in the eye. 'I didn't even know you had a brother who died until a few minutes ago.'

But they both knew that what they had shared minutes before had *not* been a stranger's kiss.

Perhaps Liam was thinking the same thing. He turned back to her. 'We're hardly strangers, Alice. It may be only a few weeks since we met, but we've shared a near-death experience and we've created a new life. How many couples achieve that in such a short time? Every relationship has its own time line.'

'But marriage is something else again. You don't know anything about marriage, Liam.' She rubbed at the carpet with the sole of a bare foot. 'Marriage isn't just about the big moments. It's day in, day out living with a person. That's when all the little things begin to matter.'

'Yes,' he agreed. 'I accept that.' His fingers traced a pattern on the arm of the chair. 'And thanks to your ex, your ability to trust your instincts has taken a battering.'

She nodded.

Liam's head dropped to one side as he frowned at her. 'You look tired. Perhaps we should talk about this some other time.'

'If you don't mind, I think I'd like to get this sorted out now. And I'm too wired to try to sleep now, anyhow.'

He waved her towards the sofa. 'Then for heaven's sake take the weight off your feet.'

Obediently, she sank into the deep chocolate velvet sofa opposite him and curled her feet beneath her.

As Liam watched her, his mouth curved in a small, sardonic smile. 'So, how far down your list are we? I must say I don't think I've ever been quite so soundly rejected.'

'Have you been rejected before?' she asked, surprised.

'Yes,' he said calmly. 'Once. It seems a long time ago now.'

He didn't seem particularly upset by the memory, but crazily enough, Alice felt jealous of the woman Liam had once loved. She wanted to ask him about her, but how could she do that when she was slap bang in the middle of yet another rejection?

'Maybe you should tell me why you think we should be married, Liam?'

His shoulders rose and fell quickly as if he'd drawn a sharp breath. And Alice wondered what had happened to her own breathing.

If Liam spoke of love, if he promised her undying devotion, her common sense would fly out the window. She would be helpless, lost in her need for him, at sea with his love as her only lifebelt.

'I want to offer you protection,' he said. 'To shield you. I hate the thought of people in the office or other business associates making you feel uncomfortable— talking about you behind your back.'

His answer was exactly what she'd expected, what she'd feared. 'That's—that's very gallant. But I'm afraid people would only talk about our shotgun wedding instead.'

In the dim lighting his eyes watched her with an intense, ferocious blaze. 'So you're determined that marriage is out of the question.'

If you don't love me. 'Yes. I'm still getting over a bad marriage experience. I need time.'

A barely perceptible tremor ran through him, shocking Alice so that she almost dashed across the room to wrap him in a bear hug.

'So,' he said, recovering quickly. 'Let's talk about alternatives.'

Somehow, alternatives didn't sound as appealing as they should have. Alice struggled to remember that she had to be sensible.

'I'm not sure what you mean by alternatives, but I must admit I'm not too keen about having everyone in the office watching me as I grow bigger and fatter with the boss's baby. I think I should resign.'

Liam frowned and his fingers drummed a tattoo on the arm of the chair. 'Don't resign. Take leave. You can take it for as long as you want. If you like, you could even do some work from home. You could concentrate on a total revamp of our outback-tour contacts.'

'OK. Actually that would be wonderful. Thank you.' She would relish having as much time as she needed to gather all the updated information from the outback-tourist options.

'What other problems do you foresee?' Liam asked her.

'I don't think there are any others that involve you.'

'I'm your baby's father. I'm involved. Get used to it, Alice.'

Well, well, she thought, Liam might be talking about fatherhood, but clearly he was back in boss-mode, supremely comfortable with making decisions and planning strategies.

'What about your family?' he asked her. 'How will they react?'

Wincing, she closed her eyes. 'I'm afraid they still haven't forgiven me for the divorce. I'm not sure how I'm going to pluck up the courage to tell them about this.'

'I'll come with you.'

Her eyes flashed open. 'No, Liam. I don't expect you to—'

'As I said, I'm involved. Get used to it. We'll take your parents to dinner somewhere tasteful and discreet and we'll tell them in a very adult and civilised manner exactly what's happened and they'll respond in an equally adult and civilised manner.'

Alice stared at him with her mouth open. Just like that he'd hit on the perfect solution. It would work. She knew it. Liam would win her parents over with his effortless charm and the aunts, too, if necessary.

'And I'd like you to meet Julia and my nephew, Jack,' he said.

Goodness, that was unexpected. Alice was gaping again. Liam had always been so secretive about his personal life.

She could sense his steely resolve. 'I'm going to help you through this, Alice.' He jumped to his feet. 'But now I really must let you get some sleep.'

Alice rose, too. She wasn't quite sure how to say goodbye; Liam had become so businesslike in the past few minutes. 'Thank you for coming.'

He was flipping open a cell-phone. 'I'll just call a cab.'

'Don't you have a car yet?' She couldn't help asking this after Shana's dark mutterings about the story in the paper.

His face turned blank. 'No, I don't need one.'

Given everything that had transpired this evening, it wasn't the moment to start quizzing Liam about why he didn't drive. But as he left her that night, dropping a light kiss on her forehead before heading outside to wait for the taxi, she realised that for all his involvement in her life, there was still a great deal she didn't know about the man.

Over the following weekend Alice cleared her desk and on Monday morning she began transforming her spare bedroom into a home office. She already had a laptop and a beautiful English oak desk that she'd had since the days when she still lived with her parents. Now she made space on the bookshelves for files, set a row of green glass tortoises on the window-sill, shopped for a cork board, a filing cabinet, a cordless phone and a new leafy pot plant to brighten the room.

Lunch was a mug of tomato soup, and an apple—for the baby.

But she was so keen to start work that she munched this at her desk. She was munching when the phone rang.

'Well done.'

'Is that you, Liam?' A piece of apple slid a little too quickly down her throat. 'What are you talking about?'

'You've just secured the long-term future of Kanga Tours.'

'I've what?'

'You've impressed the hell out of our most important potential investor—Kenny Toh from Asia-Pacific Investments.'

'Oh, Mr Toh. Yes, I remember him. He was in the office last week with his wife and daughter, on their way home to Singapore, but I didn't know he was from Asia-Pacific.'

'Apparently he did a little spying—came in with his family and posed as a tourist. And you provided him with exceptional customer service, attention to detail, courtesy, cultural awareness and professionalism.'

'Is that what he said?'

'Yes, just now, in an email.'

'Are you sure it was me?'

'Yes, he was very specific and he wants you to look after his family's bookings when they come back for a holiday. You've no idea what this means to me, Alice. Asia-Pacific is huge and I really need their backing. I spent half my time in Sydney looking after

Kenny, but he was still lukewarm when he left. Wasn't promising anything.'

'But he's definitely come on board now?'

'The contract documents for an investment agreement will be in the Sydney office tomorrow.'

'Well, that's terrific. Congratulations.'

'The congratulations are all yours. I owe this to you.'

'Well…I'm pleased,' she said, glad Liam couldn't see how broadly she was grinning.

Liam was grinning at his desk too, but his expression sobered when Dennis Ericson marched pompously through his doorway.

'Right, Conway, I want to have a word with you.'

Leaning back in his chair, Liam met his employee with a level gaze. 'I'm pleased to see you've taken advantage of my open-door policy, Dennis.'

'Well, I suspect you're planning to sack me anyhow, so I can risk speaking my mind.'

'You'd better take a seat.'

Dennis looked a little taken aback, but he sat and squared his shoulders. 'I hope you understand what a stupid, lousy thing you've done.'

Liam's right eyebrow rose. 'I'm all ears.'

'In case you haven't guessed, I'm talking about Alice. I've just heard that she's left us.'

'Alice has elected to work from home.'

'Yeah, whatever. The first phase of downsizing the staff, more likely. Look, Conway, you've just lost your best employee. Alice was the finest worker we've ever had here. She's a wonderful woman.'

Liam acknowledged this with a silent nod of his head. 'Is that the only thing upsetting you?'

'You must know it's been the talk of the office—you and her.'

'You don't approve of us?'

Dennis squared his jaw. 'Alice's husband was a bastard. And, unfortunately, some women just keep making the same mistake, over and over.'

'Is that all?'

'Not quite. Alice should never have been put in a position where she felt she had to leave us.'

Liam smiled slowly. 'That's the spirit, Dennis,' he said quietly.

The other man's jaw dropped. 'I beg your pardon?'

'What you've just said is exactly what I'd expect to hear from one of Alice's loyal friends. I'll take your comments on board.'

'B-but w-what's going to happen?'

'About?'

'Alice's position. And—and our jobs.'

'I'll get back to you. You'll be fully briefed at our staff meeting this afternoon.'

Dennis opened his mouth, but he didn't speak.

'Good morning,' said Liam, looking rather deliberately at his watch.

Dennis left with his mouth still hanging open.

'You're what?' Mary-Ann's voice was close to a squeal.

'Pregnant,' Alice repeated as she handed her friend a mug of coffee.

'But I thought you were supposed to be infertile.'

'Yeah, so did I.'

It was the end of Alice's first day of self-imposed exile and she was so pleased that Mary-Ann had called in on the way home from work.

'Oh, my God, Alice, what a shock for you.'

Alice had to laugh at the totally gobsmacked way her friend stared at her as they carried their mugs out to the back deck.

'Watch out. You're about to walk into the door post,' Alice warned her.

'Whoops.' Mary-Ann set her mug on the table and let out an amazed breath as she sank into a wicker chair. 'A baby! Wow! That's so amazing.' She fanned her face with her hand. 'Woo! It's taking me a minute or two to adjust—you and the boss. Oh, boy.'

'Yes, I know. That's exactly why I've decided to work from home. Can you imagine what it would be like if I was there in the office growing more and more pregnant with the boss's baby?'

'It would be kinda weird for him, too, when he's just arrived and is trying to establish himself,' Mary-Ann admitted. 'Thank God he's not married after all, Alice.'

'Yes,' Alice agreed fervently.

'So…how's he taking this?'

'Oh, he's adjusted to the shock quite well really.' Mary-Ann was a good friend, but Alice didn't want to go into too much detail. There was always a risk that something could slip out and her comments could get back to Liam via the staff gossip chain.

'I don't suppose there's any chance you'll get married?'

'Not in the foreseeable future.' Alice stalled further

discussion of that by posing a question of her own. 'Have I caused much of a stir in the office?'

'Oh, about 8 on the Richter Scale. Dennis was so worked up about you he went and confronted the boss.'

'Good grief.' Alice tried to picture that volatile scenario and gave up. 'What happened?'

'Actually, you won't believe it. Liam Conway's a Mystery Man all right. Just when we thought we had him worked out he surprised us again.'

'What do you mean?' Alice hoped she didn't sound too anxious. Mysteries surrounding Liam were her biggest stumbling block.

'Well…' Mary-Ann nursed her coffee mug between two hands as she warmed to her story. 'This afternoon we were all lined up for the big sermon about the future direction of the company and our job prospects and so on, and the first thing the boss did was single out Dennis.'

'Ouch. He shouldn't have gone into bat for me. I hope that wasn't the end of him?'

'No. This is what takes the cake. First, Liam gave Dennis a short, but pretty fair assessment of his shortcomings. You know—a bit aggressive, can be over-pedantic, prone to conspiracy theories. And just when we all thought Dennis was going to pack up and walk out, the boss said that Dennis's strength was that he wasn't afraid to speak his mind if it was in the best interests of the company.'

Mary-Ann paused dramatically and took a sip of her coffee.

'And?' prompted Alice. 'For heaven's sake, tell me what happened.'

'Liam promoted him.'

Alice almost dropped her mug. 'Wow.'

'Liam's sending him off on special courses in risk management and Dennis is going to be a sort of company guard dog, dealing with things like—you know—operators who might be taking short cuts with safety for our clients.'

'But that's a great idea. Dennis would be perfect.'

'I know. It was a brilliant stroke. Dennis can't wipe the grin off his face.'

Well done, Liam, Alice thought with a hint of undeserved pride. As she set down her mug, she asked, 'What about you and Shana? Any dramas there?'

'No.' Mary-Ann said this just a little too quickly. 'Actually, I don't really want to worry you, but Shana's making a bit of a fool of herself.'

Alice drew a deep breath. 'How?'

'She's hanging around Liam like you wouldn't believe. And she's volunteered to drive him so often we're thinking of buying her a chauffeur's cap.'

Alice wished she hadn't asked.

For the dinner with Alice's parents, Liam organised an impressive meal served in a private dining room at The Stapleton, the city's most prestigious hotel. He was a charming, attentive and entertaining host and Zara and Harold Madigan fell under his spell within the first few minutes. They enjoyed themselves thoroughly.

They asked for endless details about the drama of the plane landing and they looked as if they couldn't quite believe their luck that this wealthy, handsome and oh, so heroic young man had taken an interest in their cast-aside daughter.

Just the same, Alice was nervous. She had great difficulty eating and when Liam reached for her hand as her parents were finishing their desserts, she almost jumped.

'Alice and I have something important to tell you,' he said.

Her mother's face flushed with sudden excitement, and he added quickly, 'But I'm afraid I have to warn you to be prepared for a bit of a shock.'

At that Alice's heart began to beat so wildly she could hardly hear Liam above the thrumming in her ears. She stared at her dessert plate, unable to bear the sudden tension in her parents' eyes.

'Alice and I are expecting a baby,' he said.

Of course, a small commotion broke out, but Alice couldn't help admiring the delicate but firm way Liam went on to explain their dilemma. In the end her parents digested the news that their infertile daughter had rather inconveniently produced proof of fertility with surprising composure.

And when Liam went on to explain that it would be too much to expect Alice to commit to another long-term relationship so soon after her divorce, they appeared to accept that news with good grace, too.

When they hugged and kissed Alice, their happiness seemed genuine.

But she should have known that even Liam couldn't ensure that her mother wouldn't try to intervene.

Before coffee was served, Zara dragged her daughter off to the ladies' room.

'So,' she said, smiling smugly at her reflection as she applied deep coral lipstick, 'have you set a date?'

Alice groaned. 'Mum, weren't you listening? I thought you understood. Liam and I are not getting married.'

'Don't be silly, dear. That darling man's besotted with you.'

'That's not the point, Mum. You'll just have to accept that it's not happening.'

'Why ever not?'

'For the reason Liam gave you. It's too rushed. I'm not ready. It's not a public disgrace these days, you know. Everyone accepts that babies arrive out of wedlock.'

'Not in our family.' Zara's freshly painted mouth pursed into a tight, uncompromising circle as she wound her lipstick down. 'Liam's asked you to marry him, hasn't he?'

Alice groaned. 'I can't marry him. I don't know him well enough.'

Her mother blinked at her. 'Excuse me, Alice, but I hope you'll come up with a better excuse.' Zara was an ex-schoolteacher, an infamously strict schoolteacher, and right now her voice was at its frostiest. 'How can I possibly be expected to tell the rest of the family that you don't know Liam Conway well enough to marry him? You are, after all, carrying his child.'

With her arms folded across her chest, Alice leaned a hip against the marble bench top and released a desperate little sigh. 'I'm sorry if I've put you in an embarrassing position, but I'm sure you'll find a delicate way to explain my latest bombshell to the aunts.'

'But you can't be enjoying your situation.'

'I don't think a rushed wedding will make me feel any better. Let's be honest, Mum, you pushed me into marriage with Todd because you were afraid I'd end up single and pregnant.'

Zara gasped.

And Alice, who had never been game to raise that subject before, chewed her lip. But then her mother was honest enough to look guilty, which, of course, in turn made Alice feel guilty. No doubt she was a very trying daughter. She leant over and dropped a quick kiss on Zara's cheek. 'Maybe it's some kind of cosmic joke that I'm pregnant and out of wedlock now.'

There was no visible response to this.

'Anyway,' said Alice, 'I've married in haste and repented at leisure once. I don't plan to do so again.'

Reluctantly, Zara nodded. But Alice knew her mother would still want the last word.

'You're not a teenager now, so I can only assume that you know what's best,' Zara said as she slipped her lipstick and compact into her handbag. She gave her reflection a quick final inspection. 'But I can't help feeling you've been lucky enough to find the right man this time.' Her eyes met Alice's and their expression softened. 'Now you just have to find the courage to trust him.'

CHAPTER TEN

THE meeting with Liam's sister-in-law, Julia, was a much easier process. She and Alice got to know each other over Sunday lunch at Liam's apartment, while he, with his nephew Jack's help, grilled tasty reef-fish fillets on the balcony barbecue.

Julia was as warm and friendly as her appearance suggested and Alice was delighted to discover that she liked the other woman just as much as she'd hoped to.

Julia was an American, who had come to Australia as an exchange student, had stayed on when she married Liam's brother and had lived Down Under for almost twenty years.

She made Alice feel ever so welcome and she kept the conversation light, focusing mostly on her excitement about moving to Cairns with its warmer climate, which apparently suited her, and about her new house, which Liam was having altered to accommodate her wheelchair.

'And Liam's told me your wonderful news,' she added, her eyes sparkling. 'I'm tickled pink at the thought of becoming an aunt.'

'And I reckon it's pretty cool that I'm going to have a cousin at last,' chimed in Jack as he walked past, *en route* to the balcony with an icy beer for his uncle. 'Just make sure it's a boy,' he added with a cheeky grin.

'I hope you don't mind that Jack knows,' said Julia. 'Liam had an uncle-nephew chat with him—man-to-man,' she explained with a quick wink. 'He thought it was best to be upfront with him.'

'That's fine,' said Alice, but she was a little taken aback. She hadn't given much thought to her baby's extended family. One little pregnancy, she realised, was like a stone dropping into a pond; the ripples spread far and wide, touching many lives. It was a sobering thought.

'You must come to lunch with me as soon as I'm settled in there,' Julia insisted when Alice was leaving. 'Come mid-week when Liam's at work and Jack's at school and we can indulge in some in-depth girl talk.'

There was a telling light in her autumn-brown eyes as she said this and Alice was almost certain Julia wanted to talk about Liam, so on several counts the invitation was irresistible. And three weeks later, bringing a potted Cooktown orchid as a housewarming gift, Alice arrived at Julia's lovely, new, low-set home.

They ate a Thai-style calamari salad in a pretty dining room that opened out into a lush tropical garden.

'You're a wonderful cook,' Alice said, enjoying the light and crispy seafood immensely.

Julia laughed. 'I'm quite spoiled really. I have a housekeeper to take care of the boring chores, so I have time to experiment with cooking. It's almost an indulgence. Cooking and gardening are my great loves. I'm going to have so much fun in this garden.' She cast an admiring glance at the lilac-petalled, purple-throated orchid Alice had given her.

But then the brightness in Julia's smile faded and was replaced by a more serious, yet gentle expression. 'You do know what I want to talk to you about, don't you, Alice?'

Suddenly nervous, Alice began to spread butter on a bread roll. 'I presume it involves Liam?'

Julia nodded, then she gave a little laugh and shook her head. 'Actually, I don't quite know where to begin.'

'I know next to nothing about Liam's life before I met him,' Alice admitted. 'I've sensed that there are things that he doesn't find easy to talk about.'

'You're absolutely right.' Julia smoothed her napkin on her lap. 'It involves why I'm in a wheelchair and…' She broke off and looked out into the garden.

'Why Liam doesn't drive?' Alice suggested, almost dreading Julia's answer.

'Yes,' Julia said. 'Poor Liam. In the long run I think he's suffered more than any of us.'

'How can you say that, after what's happened to you?'

'I believe it's true.'

A suffocating heaviness settled over Alice, like a fog closing in. She'd been about to bite into the roll but now she set it back on the side-plate. 'So am I right in guessing there was a car accident?'

Julia nodded. 'It happened on the way to Liam and Peter's twenty-first birthday. Did you know they were twins?'

'No.' Oh, lord, no. His birthday. How awful. Alice thought of the night she had met Liam in the Hippo Bar. She'd sensed then that there was something dark behind his urge to celebrate. But his brother! A twin. Twins were always so incredibly close. Soul mates.

'How terrible for Liam,' she whispered. 'For all of you. Was—was Peter your—Jack's father?'

'Yes. We were married very young. Pete and Liam were identical twins, so they looked very alike, but my Pete was more of a comedian. He was so much fun.' Her eyes sparkled momentarily with happy memories. 'Peter Conway literally swept me off my feet. I was just nineteen.'

Alice could imagine it—the beautiful, warm, vibrant girl and a laughing, fun-loving Liam look-alike. They would have been a stunning couple.

'Liam was driving, but the accident wasn't his fault,' said Julia, suddenly serious again.

Thank God. Relief brushed across Alice. 'He must have taken some comfort from that,' she said.

'No, unfortunately he didn't. Not at all.' Julia sighed and, gripping the arms of her chair, she shifted slightly. Alice tried to imagine the awful weight of guilt that Liam must have shouldered.

'He's always blamed himself,' Julia went on. 'But it was never his fault. It was one of those awful things that just happen. An accident. We were all so excited on our way to the party and Pete was telling a riotous joke and Liam was laughing hard, so it's possible he lost concentration for a second or two. But then an old man, who didn't have right of way, drove out from a side-street straight in front of us. There wasn't much Liam could do. He tried to swerve to avoid the other car and, well, we hit a lamppost.'

Alice's throat felt as if she'd swallowed sharp glass.

'The old fellow and Liam both came away without a scratch,' said Julia. 'The accident was the other driver's fault, of course. But poor Liam has never forgiven himself. And he's turned himself inside out ever since trying to make amends.'

'He obviously cares a great deal for you,' Alice suggested.

Julia's eyes were luminous. 'I was in hospital for a year after the crash and Liam was there almost every day. My parents live in California and they were able to come over for a while, but they couldn't stay. After Jack was born by Caesarean section, it was Liam who took total responsibility for him. He brought my baby to me in the hospital—sometimes twice a day. On weekends he spent hours there, making sure Jack had every chance to get to know me as his mother.'

Alice's vision blurred as she thought of her own baby, beginning to show as the tiniest swell in her abdomen. She realised she hadn't given nearly enough thought to how Liam must feel about their child. If he'd shown extraordinary love and commitment to another couple's baby when he was twenty-one, it wasn't surprising that he'd insisted on being involved with his own.

'There's more,' Julia said, smiling gently. 'If you think you can take it.'

'I must admit it's a lot to come to grips with.' Alice tried to return Julia's smile. 'But I'm very grateful. It helps to know all this. And I can understand now why Liam hasn't been keen to talk about it.'

Julia nodded and took a sip from a frosted glass of iced tea. 'I'm almost ashamed to admit it, but the main impetus for Liam to turn himself into a mega-successful businessman was so he'd have enough money to keep Jack and me in comfort.'

Another surprise. 'Wasn't there compensation?' Alice couldn't help asking. 'From the courts?'

'Yes, eventually, but it took years. In the meantime, Liam set about making sure I had the best of everything. He wouldn't listen to my protests. He worked like the devil.' Julia noticed Alice's empty glass. 'Have some more iced tea,' she said, lifting the jug.

'Thanks.' Alice watched the tea and ice cubes swirling into her glass, but her thoughts were with Liam and her heart ached for him. What a heavy load he'd carried from such an early age.

'Julia, I probably shouldn't ask you this. But did Liam ask you to marry him?' Alice questioned gently.

Julia looked a little embarrassed. 'Bless him, yes, he did.'

'Recently?' She tried not to sound too hurt.

'No, it must be, oh, almost twelve years ago now.'

So Julia was the one, the other woman who'd rejected his marriage proposal. A long time ago.

'Why didn't you marry him?' Alice forced herself to ask.

'I knew he was doing it out of a sense of duty.'

Duty! A shiver skittered down Alice's spine. It was the same reason *she'd* rejected Liam. Not the reason she'd given him, but deep down she knew that his proposal had been prompted by a desire to 'do the right thing'. That was what worried her most. 'Did you love Liam?' she asked in a voice that was barely above a whisper.

'Not in a wifely way.' A wistful shadow flitted

across Julia's face. 'Liam is so much like Pete and yet nothing like him. Pete was an irresistible, light-hearted charmer, whereas Liam is a little more serious, deeper perhaps. I adore Liam, but never in the way I loved my rascal, Pete. I wanted to die when he died. If it wasn't for Jack—'

For the first time, Julia's sense of composure crumpled. With a little cry, Alice rose from her seat and went to hug her, and the two women clung, sharing a moment too poignant for words. When they let go, they both had tears in their eyes.

'Look at us,' laughed Julia as she wiped her eyes. 'I invite you to lunch and then launch a sob-fest.'

Alice managed to laugh too as she returned to her seat. 'You've no idea of the damage you've done,' she said.

'Oh, dear.' Julia looked worried.

'I was already in love with Liam, but after everything you've told me I think my condition is terminal.'

'But that's fabulous,' Julia cried.

Is it? Alice wondered. Not if Liam was offering to marry her out of a sense of duty, just as he had with Julia.

'I can't help wishing that Liam felt comfortable enough to tell me everything you've just told me,' she said.

'Perhaps I've jumped the gun.'

'I'm glad you've talked to me. It really helps to know.'

'Men find it harder to open up. Give Liam time, Alice. I'm sure he will want to talk to you about it, but not till he's ready.'

'Yes, well, I guess he'll have plenty of time. I've had one bad experience of marriage and it's made me ultra-cautious, so I won't allow myself to rush into anything.'

Julia nodded thoughtfully. 'I guess that's fair enough.' And then she smiled. 'If only romance could be simple and straightforward like it is in movies.'

Straightforward romance?

Was it possible? Alice wondered over the weeks that followed. Nothing seemed to be turning out right. When Liam first told her that he planned to remain involved in her life, she'd more or less expected that he would want to carry on their relationship much as it had been before. They would be a couple who went out together. While they got to know each other better they would continue to be lovers, and at some vague point in the distant future they would both decide for sure that they were ready for marriage.

But Liam, it seemed, had a different idea. He was friendly, caring, but…distant. Every so often he took her out to dinner, but he delivered her safely to her front door by taxi, and didn't accompany her inside. And then there were long periods when she didn't *see* him at all. When her mother telephoned with an invitation to Sunday lunch to introduce Liam to the other family members, Alice made excuses.

She threw herself into her work, researching relentlessly, cataloguing any possible information that tourists in the outback might want. She knew when and where magpie geese nested. She knew the best times to view the phenomenal rolling cloud formations called Morning Glory. She had every horse-riding or bike trail mapped and linked up with four-wheel drive connections.

Liam emailed or telephoned her almost every evening. They discussed the work he'd sent her and he kept her fully informed about developments in the business. Their conversations were relaxed and affable, as if they were good friends. There was no flirting. Not a breath of romance.

It was almost as if Liam planned an agenda for these calls. He engineered their conversations so that they talked about safe topics, so there was no danger of crossing into more intimate territory. They discussed the books they were reading, television shows they'd seen, current events, even politics. After her doctor's visits Liam wanted detailed reports.

Alice found herself hanging out for that daily contact, but the careful distance, the complete lack of flirting or intimate exchange hurt. Not once did Liam say, 'Missing you'.

She missed *him* desperately. She needed to see him. She needed to touch him. She didn't have so much as a photo of him and she longed for the sight of those light blue eyes and the special way he looked at her. She yearned for the warmth of his lips on her skin, the sure touch of his hands on her body.

But it was becoming unbearably clear that Liam's feelings for her had changed now that she was carrying his child. He'd developed the same mindset for her as he had for Julia. Compassion. Concern. Guilt. Duty.

In her darkest moments Alice convinced herself that Liam probably wished he'd never made love to her.

But then…she would remember the breathless passion of his lovemaking…the way he could lose himself in the wild oblivion of it. How could he regret that?

Damn him. *She* wanted it. She needed his hungry kisses, his strong shoulders, his loving hands, his lean, virile body.

On the day she felt the baby move, she decided it was time to take some action. She told him her exciting news as soon as he rang.

And she heard his excitement, too, in the sharp rasp of his indrawn breath.

'Why don't you come over, Liam? You could feel it, too. It's so cute.' She knew it was ridiculous, but she felt almost as wicked as Eve dangling the apple in front of Adam.

'Why don't you just tell me what it feels like?' he said in a dry, unreadable tone.

'Oh, it's too hard to describe.' She was stretched on the sofa, one hand gently tracing the swell of her tummy, wishing it was his hand there. 'You need to feel it for yourself.'

She waited for him to say something, and was incredibly depressed when he didn't.

'Liam?'

'I…I can't make it tonight.' He made a slight throat-clearing sound. 'Come on, Alice, tell me about it. What's it feel like?'

The tension that had been building inside her broke. 'I told you, it's too hard to put into words.' She almost hung up.

'You're angry,' he said after a stretch of prickling silence.

'Oh, so you noticed? Congratulations. Yes, I am angry. What's with you, for heaven's sake? I thought you wanted to be involved in this pregnancy. You can't expect to be involved by remote control.'

'Hang on,' he retorted just as sharply. 'I thought that was what *you* wanted. You made it patently clear you wanted me out of your hair. You told me, you told your mother, and you told Julia. Everyone seems to know that you want time and space to sort yourself out.'

'I don't need sorting out.'

'I wouldn't be too sure about that.' Was there a hint of insult in Liam's voice?

Alice bristled with mounting fury. 'What do you mean?'

'Look…' He let out a loud, impatient sigh. 'Just make up your mind on what you want, Alice. And then when you're sure, you let me know.'

'But I don't have to work anything out. I know what I want.'

'Yeah? It might be helpful if you'd fill me in.'

I want you here. I want you to love me.

Damn it. No way was she going to beg for his love.

When she didn't answer, Liam sighed again. 'Alice, I'm going out of my way to handle this exactly the way you want it.'

'Well, you could have fooled me.' Livid with him for not understanding what was so perfectly obvious to her, Alice slammed the phone down. And burst into tears.

Maybe it was her hormones; they'd been making her a bit teary, but now she totally gave in to them. Curled in a ball, she sobbed her aching heart out.

How could Liam be so dumb? How could he possibly think she wanted to be left alone, to never see him? Damn the man. He'd made her pregnant. And now he was staying clear of her, making her miserable and lonely while delivering lectures about sorting herself out! What would he know?

Thank heavens she'd never accepted his proposal of marriage.

Oh, my God. Alice uncurled abruptly and sat up as something fell into place in her scrambled thoughts...

On the night Liam had come to her, worried because she was ill, and she'd told him she was pregnant—what was the first thing he'd done?

He'd asked her to marry him. He'd taken her into his arms and he'd kissed her tenderly and he'd proposed marriage.

And what had she done? She'd pulled away from him. She'd leapt out of his arms and become businesslike. She'd refused his offer and told him in no uncertain terms that she needed time to recover from the breakdown of her first marriage.

Was the man taking her literally?

She thought about it. He'd kept his word to the letter. He'd taken her on polite, almost formal dates. He'd spoken to her parents, he'd introduced her to his family, and he'd stayed involved—from a distance. Oh, good heavens, was this *her* fault?

Looking at this from Liam's point of view, he had every right to be furious with her. She'd laid down the law, he'd followed it, and then she'd told him he was doing it all wrong. And hung up on him.

Now she'd stuffed things up completely. Liam

Conway was not the sort of guy you hung up on. He would probably never telephone her again.

When the telephone rang she jumped. Oh, cringe, she was in no state to talk to anyone now.

'Hello.' Her nose was stuffy from crying and she needed to blow it.

'Are you OK?'

It was Liam. The concern in his voice was so sweet she almost burst into more tears. She turned her head from the receiver and tried to sniff quietly. 'Liam, before you say anything—I'm so sorry about hanging up.' Her voice sounded pathetically teary.

'You've been crying.'

'I've stopped now.' She sniffed again. 'Don't worry about me.'

'Huh, you've got to be joking.'

He was trying to sound casual, but there was an anxious undertone that tore her heart to shreds.

'Everything I said before was wrong, Liam. Instead of giving you an earful, I should have told you that I—I miss you. I miss you so much.'

There was a beat of silence. 'I thought you wanted to take a step back—so you could get some perspective.'

'I know, I know. I laid down the law and you've been trying to do the right thing and now I'm acting like a spoiled princess because I don't like my own rules.'

She fancied she heard the softest of chuckles.

'I wouldn't put it quite like that,' he said. 'But you are, after all, a pregnant princess, so why don't you adjust the rules to suit yourself?'

'This should be a two-way thing.'

'Well, yeah, I agree.' There was a pause, and then, 'I can be as close to you as you want me, Alice.'

As close as you want me… Just as well she was sitting down, she went straight into meltdown. 'Oh— um, that—sounds—well, I'd love to see you.'

'When? Where?'

Here. Now.

Whoa. Calm down. Take a deep breath. It was mega-important to get this right, to handle things calmly. Inviting Liam to her house was how this had all begun. 'How about—um—an outing, then?' Good grief, she sounded so prim, like one of her aunts. 'What about a picnic?'

Actually, she'd been fantasising for weeks about taking Liam up into the mountains, finding a quiet clearing in a rainforest. She could picture it all—Liam stretched out beside her on a picnic rug, where she could feast her eyes on him, touch him.

'A picnic? Where?'

'Kuranda. It's gorgeous up at the top of the range. There are craft markets and the rainforest is just beautiful. And we can take the Skyrail.'

Bless Julia for telling her about Liam's accident. She didn't want to add tension to their date by insisting on a car journey.

'The Skyrail's brilliant. It takes you right across the rainforest canopy,' she added. 'Actually, we could take it one way and come back down the range by the scenic railway. I'll bring a picnic lunch and we can breathe some mountain air and take a walk in the rainforest and just kick back.'

'You've convinced me. It's a terrific idea. When? Tomorrow's Saturday. Is that too soon?'

'Tomorrow's fine.' Fine? It was fantastic. 'I'll see you in the morning.'

This time, as she hung up, she let out a little *whoop* of triumph. A whole day with Liam. At last.

CHAPTER ELEVEN

IT RAINED the next morning. The storm started early, not long after midnight—a proper tropical downpour with thunder and lightning and rain thick as rope. By eight-thirty, when Liam was due to arrive, the heavy rain showed no signs of letting up.

In a cloud of gloom Alice waited for the phone call that would tell her he wasn't coming. After all, what was the point? They would see nothing from the Skyrail, and a picnic was impossible.

But there was no phone call. And at eight-thirty-two, a taxi pulled up outside her flat and a big, shiny black umbrella and a pair of long, blue jeans-clad legs dashed up her front path.

She threw open her door and there was Liam, looking only slightly damp and good enough to eat.

'I thought you might not come.' She knew she was grinning madly.

'Couldn't break our date.' He grinned back at her.

What a pair of grinning fools they were.

'Well, come on in,' she said, as a gust of wind brought water scudding across her little porch. 'At least I can make you some coffee.'

They went through to her kitchen. Feeling strangely nervous, she tried to look busy, attending to the coffee-pot, mugs, sugar, but as she worked she could see Liam in her periphery, coming closer.

He took her by the shoulders, gently turned her to

face him and he let his gaze travel over her. 'Wow, it's happening so quickly, isn't it? You're really starting to look pregnant.'

'Yes.' Shyly she used both hands to flatten her pale green top to show off the new curve of her abdomen. 'See what you've been missing out on?'

She felt a rush of goose-pimples when she saw the sudden sheen in his eyes and the way his throat worked.

'It's happened all of a sudden,' she hurried to explain. 'Just this past week I've had to buy looser clothes.'

'So, how big would the baby be now?'

'Ooh, about fourteen centimetres.'

He held his hands out in front of him, trying to calculate the distance. 'That's still pretty tiny.'

'Yes, but it has eyelashes and eyebrows. And it even has tastebuds on its tongue.'

'Tastebuds? No kidding?' He grinned again. 'So you're keeping close tabs on what's going on in there.'

'Of course. I have a whole shelf of books that give me week-by-week progress notes. The trouble is I get impatient. I keep wanting to rush on to the next stage.'

She turned back to the coffee machine and Liam made himself at home, with his hips settled against her kitchen cupboards, his arms folded across his chest and one foot crossed casually in front of the other. 'I wonder if it's a boy or a girl.'

'I'll be having an ultrasound next week.' She flicked the switch on her electric kettle to boil water for a cup of herbal tea, because she wasn't drinking coffee these days. 'They might be able to tell me the baby's sex.' Her eyes met his. 'They give you a choice—whether or not you want to know. Would you like to?'

His eyebrows shot high as he thought about this. 'I'm not sure,' he said. 'Do you want to?'

Right at that moment all Alice could think was how wonderful it was to have Liam here, to be able to see him while she had this conversation.

Afraid that her feelings might be shining too obviously, she turned quickly to the fridge and reached for the milk. 'I can't decide.' She set the milk on the counter. 'Maybe not.'

'The suspense of not knowing is kind of fun,' he suggested.

She nodded. 'Part of me desperately wants to know, but I like the idea of getting a surprise at the end, too.'

She looked at him again and he smiled such a gorgeous, knee-weakening smile that it took all her willpower not to throw herself at him.

'Do you have a preference? Boy or girl?' he asked.

'Not really.' The kettle boiled and she poured water into a small teapot. 'Actually, that's a lie,' she said, smiling shyly. 'I want a boy.' *A boy just like you, Liam.* 'What about you?'

'Well…' The skin around his eyes crinkled. 'I'm rather hoping it's a little girl.'

Alice laughed. 'Then maybe it would be best if I ask them not to tell me, so we can both keep hoping.'

She glanced at the counter where she'd set the picnic basket last night, ready to be packed this morning. 'While you're here, I should make the most of your height. Could you put this basket back up on top of that cupboard?'

'Sure.' As Liam picked it up, he frowned at her. 'How did you get it down?'

'I have a little stepladder.'

'For crying out loud, Alice, you shouldn't be climbing ladders.'

'It was only a couple of steps. I'm pregnant, Liam, not porcelain.' Just the same, she was happy to let him stow the basket away, especially as it gave her a chance to watch the way the muscles in his arms rippled and the way his jeans hugged his behind as he reached up.

'You wouldn't like to do that five or six times would you?' she asked.

He turned back to her, his eyes signalling amusement. 'You were taking a good look, were you?'

She gave an offhand shrug, but she couldn't suppress a dimpling smile. 'Maybe.'

For long seconds they stood facing each other. In the tense silence her eyes lingered on his face. She saw him swallow and heard the kitchen clock ticking, the coffee machine bubbling and her heartbeats picking up pace.

Then everything seemed to happen in an instant. Liam quickly crossed the room and switched off the coffee, and then stepped towards her, scooped her in…and kissed her.

Hard. Wonderfully hard.

It was a kiss so sudden and passionate that it left her senses reeling. She clung to him, drowning in pleasure, dimly aware that time and distance had only served to make their need for each other stronger and fiercer than ever.

She'd dreamed of this in the past lonely weeks—his hungry kiss, with his mouth crushing hers, his tongue pushing her lips apart and his hands hauling her closer and closer.

She revelled in the ferocity of it, the raw, desperate need. His hands travelled over her, her hands travelled over him, kneading his shoulders, glorying in their solid masculinity, exploring the muscles in his back, then she riffled her fingers through his short, springy hair before settling at last with her arms about his neck as she pressed her soft curves into his hard maleness, straining to be as close as possible.

When Liam released her he stood very still, the colour high in his face. 'I suppose I should apologise,' he said.

Shaking her head, she offered him an uncertain smile. 'In case you didn't notice, I rather liked it.'

'But as you very rightly pointed out once before, it was sex that got us into trouble.'

'I'm not in trouble.' She looked down and gave her tummy a light pat. 'The only troubling thing about my—*situation* is that I've had to live without you. I'm finding that very difficult. Impossible actually.'

She lifted her gaze and saw the way Liam was looking at her, and she forgot to breathe.

'I've missed you terribly,' she said and she let out an embarrassed little huff and looked away.

'Yeah, well, that's mutual.' With his hands he cradled her face and turned her to look at him. His thumbs traced the lines of her cheekbones.

'I can't believe we got our wires crossed so badly,'

she said, thrilled by the gentle caress. Lifting her hand, she covered his, holding it against her skin. 'How could you think I'd be happy without this? I can't survive with just phone calls.'

His shrug was accompanied by a rueful smile. 'I was letting you call the tune, but don't worry, I wasn't going to wait much longer.'

'Well,' said Alice, deciding suddenly that if she was going to call the tune, she would make her message clear as a bell. 'I think that what I'm actually telling you when I say that I missed you—what I actually mean is I—I love you.'

'Alice!' Liam enfolded her in his arms again, but more gently this time.

'I understand that you may not love me back,' she told his shoulder.

He leaned away, so that he could look at her. 'What gave you that idea? I've known since I was in Sydney that I was desperately in love with you.'

'Since Sydney?'

'I should have put it on the card.'

'The card you sent with the beautiful green bowl?'

He picked up a strand of her hair, curling it around his forefinger. 'I wanted to tell you then how I felt, but apart from the fact that I was so damn busy that I had to get my PA to write the card, I decided it would be better to tell you in person, just as soon as I got back.'

'But you didn't.' Alice gave his chest a little push. 'When you came to my flat, when you asked me to marry you, you didn't say a single thing about love. You just talked a lot of high-minded stuff about wanting to protect me.'

Liam grimaced. 'Yeah. You see…there were some…*things* I needed to tell you first, but you had your own problems to sort through and I didn't want to burden you with mine.'

'I know about the accident, Liam.'

He seemed to freeze.

'Julia told me,' she said, her voice barely above a whisper. She could see visible tension working in his jaw, in his neck and in his clenching fist. 'I hope you don't mind that I know.'

'No.' He drew a deep breath. 'I was planning to tell you, but Julia has always had a better sense of timing than I do.' The tension in his face gave way to a smile. 'You know I had an engagement ring in my pocket on that night I came to you?'

She was so shocked she stepped backwards out of his arms. 'An engagement ring? You mean you were planning to propose even before—even, oh, heck, *before* you knew I was pregnant?'

'I was considering it.'

She couldn't believe it. If she'd hadn't been so screwed up, so obsessed about her divorce…if she'd given Liam just a chance to get his feelings out…

'If I'd been sensible,' said Liam, 'I probably would have proposed to you on the first night we met.'

'In the Hippo Bar?'

His smile had the uneasy self-consciousness of an endearing little boy. 'I reckon that's when I began falling in love with you. Actually, I think it probably happened the moment I set eyes on you, even before we started sampling Screaming Orgasms.'

Alice stared at him, stunned.

'You don't believe me?'

'I don't know. Well, yes, I'm only too happy to believe you, but I—I can't get my head around the idea that you've had an engagement ring all this time.'

'So,' he said, taking a sudden, deep breath, 'is it too soon to ask you if you'd accept the ring?'

Linking her hands behind his neck again, she leaned in to kiss him. 'Liam Conway, I don't deserve you.'

He placed a finger over her lips. 'Stop thinking that way. You deserve a man who worships you.'

'Well, you deserve happiness and my baby and I want to make you happy, Liam.'

He brushed warm lips across her brow. 'Say that you'll accept my ring and I'll be a happy man.'

'Of course I'll accept it.'

'Without seeing it first?'

'Of course.' But then curiosity got the better of her. 'What's it like?'

He grinned. 'Not telling. I'll keep it as a surprise.'

She wrinkled her nose at him. 'Spoilsport.' Then, not wanting to mar this beautiful moment, she hastened to reassure him. 'Actually, I'd be blissfully happy if your ring was a piece of scratched glass set in plastic.'

'It's a little better than that,' he said. 'I think it's beautiful. As soon as I saw it I thought of you. The colour, the setting—it seemed perfect.'

She waggled her ring finger. 'But do you know if it will fit me?'

He grabbed her hand and made an exaggerated study, frowning as he examined her ring finger from several angles. 'Hmm. We could have a problem.'

'It doesn't really matter if the ring's the wrong size.'

Liam's eyes were dancing. 'It might be a bit big, but they can do wonderful things these days.'

'Yes, it's easy enough to reduce the ring.'

'No, Alice. Haven't you heard? They've worked out a way to enlarge your finger.'

She landed a playful punch on his shoulder.

'OK,' he said, laughing. 'Why don't we settle this now by going over to my place to check the ring out?'

Alice grinned. 'Why not?' She glanced out the window to the grey rain sheeting down. 'There's no chance of a picnic.'

'Once you've seen the ring we can spend a long afternoon thinking up interesting rainy-day activities.'

'Mmm.' She felt deliciously lusty just thinking about it. 'Sounds wonderful. We'll take my car?'

'OK.'

'I'll get my things.'

Alice couldn't believe how absolutely ecstatic she was as she hurried through to her bedroom. Quickly she checked the contents of her shoulder bag. Her purse, driver's licence and hair comb were there, as well as the hundred and one things a girl needed on any given day.

Oh, and she'd better make a quick trip to the bathroom.

These days she needed to go more often.

But in the bathroom she stared in horror.

Oh, God, no.

There were dark spots on her underwear.

A surge of pure panic shot through her and her heart began to bang like a loose shutter in a storm.

'Liam!' she cried, rushing back to the kitchen.

'You've gone so pale. What's the matter?'

'I'm spotting.'

'You're what?' Another look at the wild terror in her eyes and he seemed to comprehend. 'Not the baby?'

'There's blood.'

The shock on his face mirrored her own quaking fear. 'Oh, hell, Alice, all of this has been too much of a shock for you.'

'A shock?' What was he talking about? 'No, no, it's not that. It's all been a wonderful surprise.'

But he didn't look convinced. 'How bad is it?'

'I—I don't know.' She tried not to sound panicky, but it wasn't possible to be brave about this. 'Oh, Liam, I don't want to lose this baby.' She felt suddenly sick, dizzy.

Liam's face was contorted with anguish as he dragged a chair across the floor. 'Here, quickly, sit down.'

'I'm probably panicking about nothing.' She looked up at him. 'But I am a bit scared.'

'You need to get to a hospital.'

She nodded. 'Could you call for a taxi? I don't think I'm up to driving.'

He scowled as he glanced towards the telephone. 'A taxi on a wet Saturday in a place like this could take too long. We'll use your car.'

'OK. I'm just a little giddy, but give me a few minutes and I should be all right to drive.'

'Hell, no, Alice. Don't even think about it.'

'But—'

White-faced, Liam crossed the room to the little

row of keys hanging near her pantry cupboard. 'These are your car keys, aren't they?'

'Yes, and the silver one is the house key, but I don't expect you to drive.'

'I'm driving you to the hospital, Alice. Now let's get going.'

He took her by the elbow to help her to her feet. 'Liam, I know you don't drive.'

He sent her a shaky smile. 'Come on, this is an emergency, Alice.'

'But are you sure you want to do this? It—it's not as if our lives are at risk like they were in the plane.'

He slipped his arm around her shoulders. 'My darling girl, the little life you're carrying is just as precious.'

Shepherding her forward, he said, 'Trust me, Alice. I promise I'll take care of you.'

Still she hesitated, but then she looked up at the blaze of fierce love in Liam's eyes and she understood with a burst of clarity that, however hard this might be for him, Liam wanted to drive her, he needed to do this.

His courage enkindled her inner faith. Yes, of course she would trust him. She'd seen how competently he'd landed an aircraft in an emergency. She was quite certain that Liam Conway was a master of every enterprise he undertook.

And she realised with a rush of confidence that from this moment on and in every way she would trust this man—on this short car journey, and with the rest of her life.

With her baby's life.

She felt calm as she smiled up at him, and as they

shared his umbrella on the journey to the car. They'd made this baby together and together they'd do everything to protect it.

Her sense of calm deepened as Liam slid into position behind the steering wheel. And then, as he adjusted the seat to accommodate his long legs and turned on the ignition, she knew he would be just fine.

Liam died a thousand deaths at the hospital.

He'd been OK while he was driving. The woman he loved had needed his help, their tiny, helpless baby needed him—and that was enough. He'd driven the car safely through driving rain and across the city without mishap.

But although he was grateful that he hadn't let Alice down, it wasn't a moment for triumph. Now he was watching a hospital orderly wheel her to an examination room. Down a long corridor. Away from him.

He caught a last glimpse of her pale, frightened face and then she was gone. And he was seized by a black, harrowing loneliness greater than any he'd ever experienced.

Oh, dear God, how could he stand this? Why had he kissed Alice so wildly? Was it possible that her problem might somehow be his fault? Alice couldn't lose her baby. He couldn't be responsible for another death. No, please, no. Not again.

His throat tightened over what felt like a sharp rock. Alice meant more to him than she could possibly guess. In the short time he'd known her, she had succeeded where his hard work, his business success and his efforts to help Julia and Jack had failed. Nothing else could push away the darkness and heal the hurt inside him. Alice had. That old chestnut about love lighting up your life was damn right.

As for her baby...*their* baby; that fourteen-centimetre being with eyelashes and eyebrows and tastebuds had already captured his heart completely.

Thrusting his hands deep into his pockets, Liam paced the polished floor. He walked to a window and looked out into the bleak grey yard. On the far side of the car park palm trees bowed to the wind, their heavy fronds waving haplessly as rain lashed at them. Flowers, pink, yellow and red, and heavy with rain, had fallen from the hibiscus bushes that lined the drive and they lay sodden and battered on the bitumen.

The sight depressed him and he moved to a stand of colourful magazines and flicked through one or two, taking in nothing.

He paced again, thinking wretchedly about Alice, alone in there with those medical people. What was happening? What were they doing to her? Was she frightened?

This was worse than all the times he'd worried about Julia.

'Mr Conway?'

He turned at the voice. A nurse seemed to have appeared out of thin air.

'Yes?' Liam felt cold all over.

She smiled. What did *that* mean? He couldn't tell if it was a smile that signalled good news or sympathy. His heart pounded.

'Dr O'Brien wants to take some ultrasound pictures of the baby and Alice would like you to be with her.'

'Right.' The single word jammed in his throat.

'It's this way,' the nurse said, heading back down the corridor.

'Thank you.' Hurrying after her, he considered asking her if there was a problem, but they arrived at their destination too quickly.

'She's in here,' the nurse said, taking a sudden turn to the left.

Too late for questions, he hurried through the door.

Alice had changed into a hospital gown and she was lying on a bed and talking to a rather serious-faced man, presumably a doctor. A technician at the end of the bed was busily adjusting a monitor screen.

Alice smiled when she saw Liam and she beckoned him closer.

He crossed quickly to her and took her hand in his. It felt cold. 'How are you?' His voice sounded rough and choked.

'I'm feeling fine,' she said. 'Liam, this is Dr O'Brien. Doctor, this is Liam Conway, the baby's father.'

'How do you do?' The two men shook hands.

'So is everything OK?' Liam dared to ask.

Dr O'Brien frowned. 'There's no immediate cause for alarm. Spotting is not uncommon. Alice's symptoms are mild and there don't seem to be any other signs of trouble, so there's a good chance she'll be perfectly fine. But we're going to do an ultrasound scan so we can check the foetal development.'

'Yes, of course,' Liam said. 'Do whatever you have to.' He wished he felt as calm as Alice looked. The poor woman needed his moral support and he was falling apart inside.

She squeezed his hand. 'Don't worry, darling.'

He forced a grin. But the grin wavered as the technician lifted her gown aside and began to spread gel on her abdomen.

Alice looked up at him and her grey eyes seemed huge as she held his hand. She smiled, but when the doctor took up a position near the screen and the technician began to move a transducer over her he could see the slightest tremor in her chin.

Liam's heart pounded. No one in the room spoke. The only sound was an occasional beep from the equipment and Liam decided there and then that landing a plane without any prior experience was a hell of a lot less stressful than becoming a first-time father.

He struggled to think of something to say—a lighthearted comment that would distract Alice from worrying about her baby. All he could think was how much he loved her—and her baby. How precious they both were.

He looked down at her hand in his and massaged her fingers with his thumb. 'When you're out of here,' he told her softly, 'we'll have to go straight to my place so I can show you that ring.'

'Oh, yes,' she said. 'I'll hold you to that. I can't wait to see it.'

More beeps sounded from the machine and Liam wished the doctor would say something.

'Actually,' said Alice, 'I think I can guess what colour it is.'

He gently jiggled her hand. 'So you're a mind reader, are you?'

'Perhaps.' She looked up at him with a shaky smile. 'I'm sure it's beautiful. If it's as tasteful as that lovely bowl you bought me, it'll be—'

'Well, well, well.' The doctor's voice interrupted her.

Alice's hand tightened around Liam's. Her eyes were huge. 'Is the baby all right?'

'I'll turn this screen and you can see for yourself.'

Liam swallowed as he stared at the monitor and tried to make sense of the blurred black and white images.

He glanced to Alice and she seemed as puzzled as he was. 'I—I can only see— What are those two circles?' Her mouth dropped open. 'Oh, my goodness, are they w-what I think they are?'

'What you're seeing here, my dear, are two little heads.' The doctor beamed at her as he pointed at the screen. 'You have two babies. And from what I can see here, both babies appear to be perfectly healthy.'

'Twins?' A smile of pure delight broke over Alice's face. She looked up. 'Liam, what do you think of that?'

He was too stunned to respond.

'You're probably not surprised, are you?' she said.

But he was. Totally. *Twins.* His mind seemed to have frozen and he couldn't tell whether he thought this was good news or bad news. His first thought was for his brother, Peter, and, as always, he felt a swift shaft of pain.

But then he forced his mind past Peter's death to remember their childhood and the fun they'd had growing up together. Peter had been his best friend, his mate. On their parents' orchard farm they'd run wild. They'd been constant companions, building forts, or tree-houses, scheming pranks, playing cricket, kicking footballs, helping each other with homework. He'd never been lonely.

'Liam?' Alice was watching him anxiously. 'You don't mind that it's twins, do you?'

He blinked. 'No, of course I don't mind. It's wonderful. It's more than wonderful. It's fantastic.'

'I think we can determine their sex, too,' said the doctor as he peered at a different image on the screen. 'Would you like to know?'

Alice was looking at Liam again. 'Would you?'

'I don't mind either way. This should be your choice, sweetheart.'

It only took her a few seconds to make up her mind. 'No,' she said, shaking her head emphatically. 'I don't want to know now, because it doesn't really matter whether they're boys or girls.' She squeezed Liam's hand. 'We already love them anyway, don't we, darling?'

Liam wanted to kiss her right there and then.

Soon after that, the procedure was completed and Liam was asked to wait outside in the corridor again while Alice went to a cubicle to change back into her own clothes.

She came out looking flushed and shiny-eyed with happiness.

'You clever girl,' he told her.

'Can you believe we're having twins?'

'The idea is slowly sinking in.'

She laughed. 'It's not a bad effort for a girl who thought she couldn't get pregnant, is it?'

'Two babies will be a handful.'

She gave his arm a gentle shake. 'We'll cope.'

Then she pulled a face. 'Of course, it means I'm going to grow as big as two houses.'

'You'll still be beautiful.'

'But you're right,' she admitted. 'Two babies will keep me busy.' Suddenly she looked troubled. 'This is not the best way to start a marriage, Liam. I want our marriage to be romantic.'

Taking her hands in his, he said, 'We'll make time for romance.' He rubbed the backs of her hands with his thumbs. 'Besides, I'd much rather be inside a marriage with you and your babies than locked on the outside without you.'

Her eyes glistened. 'Don't worry. The babies and I insist on having you there with us—on the inside.'

He smiled and bent his head to drop two warm kisses on her happy lips. 'That's a kiss for each of your babies.'

Her cheeks dimpled. 'And what about another one for their mother, please?'

'Just a gentle one this time. I don't want to get you all stirred up again.'

'Liam, stop worrying and kiss me. Properly.'

He glanced up and down the corridor. 'Isn't it rather public here?'

'Be quick, then.'

Liam obeyed. 'You have no idea how much I love you, Alice.'

'I love you, too,' she said close to his ear. 'And your babies. We're going to be all right, Liam. I'm sure of it.'

As they headed down the corridor, Alice stopped again, abruptly. 'Goodness, I've totally overlooked thanking you for driving me here.'

His mouth twisted into a crooked smile. 'No big deal.'

But they both knew what an understatement that was. In many ways that short car journey had been a private symbol of faith and commitment for both of them.

'And now,' Liam said, 'I'm going to drive you to my place. The doctor told me you still have to take things quietly for the next few days. You're going to put your feet up and you're going to allow me to pamper you with dainty morsels while you admire your engagement ring.'

She slipped her arm through the crook of his elbow. 'Now, that sounds like my kind of Saturday.'

CHAPTER TWELVE

SHE was sitting alone at the bar with her back to him, but she knew the moment he arrived. She saw his reflection in the mirror behind the bar and a *frisson* of anticipation danced across her skin as she watched him make his way towards her.

When he drew close their eyes met in the mirror—hers clear grey, his light blue. He smiled and she smiled back at him—a private exchange between a man and a woman in love.

When he slipped onto the stool beside her, she turned his way and warmth began to pool deep inside her. It was two years to the day since she'd met this man here in this bar, and his face was now as familiar as her own, but nothing could dim her desire for him.

'Hi there,' he said, his blue eyes making a leisurely, yet appreciative inspection of her sleeveless dress of smoky green silk. It was new and slinky and she was pleased that he liked it.

'Hi,' she said simply.

With his elbows resting on the bar, he leaned close and whispered in her ear, 'Has anybody ever told you, you're bloody beautiful?'

'Mmm,' she murmured, the warmth spreading through her as she watched the flare of heat in his eyes. 'My husband tells me all the time.'

'Glad to hear it,' he said, straightening once more.

'So he should.' He turned his attention to the glass she was holding. 'What are you drinking?'

'Angels' Tears.'

He looked surprised. 'Not a Screaming Orgasm?'

Her eyes sparkled cheekily. 'I don't need to buy one. My husband serves them up at home any time I want.'

This time the smile they exchanged was highly charged.

But then she set down her glass and gave his arm a gently reproachful shove. 'Maybe coming here wasn't such a good idea, Liam. If you keep flirting like this I'll have to take you home to bed and that would be a terrible waste of a night out, especially as I'm breaking in new babysitters.'

He grinned. 'So what are you saying? You want me on my best behaviour?'

'No,' she admitted, looking sheepish.

'We can talk about this afternoon's board meeting if you like.'

'Not tonight.'

'That's a relief. I'd much rather—'

The barman arrived then and asked for Liam's order and he chose a beer. They waited while the frosty glass was filled and Alice glanced at her left hand, at the slim gold wedding band and the beautiful engagement ring, an emerald surrounded by diamonds. She smiled, remembering that it had been a perfect fit the very first time Liam had slipped it on her finger.

'Cheers,' Liam said, clinking his brimming glass against hers. 'Happy birthday, darling.'

'Happy birthday, Liam.'

They shared a light, flirtatious kiss.

'You know,' Liam said after he'd taken a sip of his drink, 'for years I used to dread this day.'

'Too many bad memories.'

'Yeah.' He stared at his beer for a moment and then looked straight at Alice. 'You've brought the balance back into my life, birthday girl. Apart from every other way that you've made me happy, you've given me a host of reasons to always feel good about this anniversary.'

She placed her hand on his. 'And you must know that you're my all-time favourite birthday present.'

It was so hard to believe now that there'd ever been a time when she was afraid to risk a second chance at marriage. From the day she and Liam exchanged their wedding vows, surrounded by family and friends on a tropical beach at sunset, her second marriage had been different from her first in every way.

Of course, that was partly because pregnancy and the birth of the twins had played such a dominant role in their newly married lives. But she and Liam had accepted the mantle of parenthood with wholehearted enthusiasm.

And they'd managed snippets of precious time alone, too, thanks to an abundance of willing baby-sitters—Julia, Zara, Mary-Ann and the aunts, as well as a paid housekeeper. Even Jack wanted to be in-volved. He'd totally forgiven Alice for not giving birth to boys and every Saturday morning he pushed his twin cousins in their double stroller while he jogged along the Esplanade.

But tonight Liam's parents were doing the baby-sitting honours. They were rapt in their new grand-children and had travelled north to Cairns so many times in the past fifteen months that they were seriously thinking about selling up their farm and moving here permanently, especially as Julia and Jack were so settled now.

'Were the girls asleep when you left?' Liam asked.

'Your father was still singing nursery rhymes to Cate, but your mother's very proud of herself. She got Lily to sleep in five minutes flat.'

Liam laughed. 'That's got to be a record. Well done, Granny Conway.'

'Of course, now your mother's hoping Lily will wake up again, so she can have another cuddle,' Alice added.

'Well…if, by some miracle, the girls sleep right through, there'll be plenty of chances for cuddles in the morning.'

Puzzled, Alice frowned at him. 'You sound as if you don't intend to be home in the morning.'

Her husband's eyes sparkled. 'Much as I adore being woken at six a.m. by my sweet little daughters, I need their mother to myself tonight.' The light in his eyes deepened. 'All night and till well after breakfast.'

Her insides felt hot and tight. 'You've planned something.'

The light in his eyes deepened as he pulled a key from his pocket and dangled it in front of her. She tilted her head in an attempt to read the name engraved on the platinum tag.

'Does that say "Cupid" something?'

'Uh-huh, this is the key to Cupid's Cave, the honeymoon suite at The Stapleton. It's brand-new, has a bed the size of a small cottage, French champagne on ice, a spa overlooking the ocean, gourmet room service. In the industry they're claiming it's the best honeymoon suite in the southern hemisphere.'

'Wow! I'm getting steamy just thinking about it.' A whole night alone with Liam was a luxury in itself.

Liam set the key on the bar and, with a teasing smile, he said, 'Of course, we could always go dancing.'

Alice grabbed the key. 'Not tonight. We can't let the newlyweds have all the fun. Come on, darling, let's go.'

MILLS & BOON®

Live the emotion

Tender romance™

THE WEDDING ARRANGEMENT *by Lucy Gordon*

(The Rinucci Brothers)

Luke is startled to discover that the tenant of his Rome *residenza*, Minnie Pepino, is young, blonde and sensational! They have an immediate attraction, but Minnie holds back, unable to let go of her past. Luke is determined to be the one man who can make her life whole again…

HIS INHERITED WIFE *by Barbara McMahon*

Inheriting half of her late husband's company means Shannon Morris is now Jase Pembrooke's business partner – to their mutual dismay! They are forced to confront their growing attraction. But Jase promised her husband he'd take care of her, and Shannon doesn't want a relationship based on obligation…

MARRIAGE REUNITED *by Jessica Hart*

(To Have and To Hold)

Georgia Henderson once had a loving husband. But his demanding career kept him away from home. With her marriage behind her, Georgia's life changed completely. Now, sending divorce papers to Mac brings him hotfooting it back to her – determined to prove that he *can* be the husband she needs…

O'REILLY'S BRIDE *by Trish Wylie* (9 to 5)

Sean O'Reilly has become so close to his colleague Maggie Sullivan that he's beginning to imagine their friendship can be more. Only – bizarrely – she's backed off. And, even more strangely, she's looking for love on the internet! Well, if Sean can't beat them, he'll have to join them…

On sale 3rd March 2006

*Available at WHSmith, Tesco, ASDA, Borders, Eason,
Sainsbury's and most bookshops*

www.millsandboon.co.uk

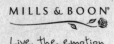

MILLS & BOON®

Live the emotion

Sweet Revenge

When passion gets out of control!

In March 2006, By Request brings back three favourite romances by our bestselling Mills & Boon authors:

Rome's Revenge by Sara Craven
The Sweetest Revenge by Emma Darcy
A Seductive Revenge by Kim Lawrence

Make sure you buy these irresistible stories!

On sale 3rd March 2006

Available at WHSmith, Tesco, ASDA, Borders, Eason, Sainsbury's and most bookshops
www.millsandboon.co.uk

0206/05a

MILLS & BOON®
Live the emotion

Medical
romance™

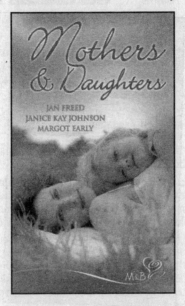

FREE

4 BOOKS AND A SURPRISE GIFT!

We would like to take this opportunity to thank you for reading this Mills & Boon® book by offering you the chance to take FOUR more specially selected titles from the Tender Romance™ series absolutely FREE! We're also making this offer to introduce you to the benefits of the Reader Service™—

★ **FREE home delivery**
★ **FREE gifts and competitions**
★ **FREE monthly Newsletter**
★ **Books available before they're in the shops**
★ **Exclusive Reader Service offers**

Accepting these FREE books and gift places you under no obligation to buy; you may cancel at any time, even after receiving your free shipment. Simply complete your details below and return the entire page to the address below. You don't even need a stamp!

YES! Please send me 4 free Tender Romance books and a surprise gift. I understand that unless you hear from me, I will receive 6 superb new titles every month for just £2.75 each, postage and packing free. I am under no obligation to purchase any books and may cancel my subscription at any time. The free books and gift will be mine to keep in any case.

N6ZEE

Ms/Mrs/Miss/Mr...................................Initials ....
BLOCK CAPITALS PLEASE

Surname ....

Address ....

....

....Postcode ....

Send this whole page to:
The Reader Service, FREEPOST CN81, Croydon, CR9 3WZ